A Shadow Jumper Mystery Adventure

Twilight Robbery

J M Forster

Cover design by Rachel Lawston

lawstondesign.com

Praise for J. M. Forster

Shadow Jumper

'Fantastically exciting. A GOLD MEDAL WINNER!'

The Wishing Shelf Book Awards

'Perfect for both teens and preteens.

Families Rating 6 out of 6.'

Families Online

'A tale full of adventure and mystery . . . with direct,

accessible language . . . A warm, human tale of friendship.'

Primary Times, Gloucestershire, UK

Bad Hair Days

'a gripping, emotional, sensitively written read'

Felicity Grace Terry

Pettywitter.blogspot.com

'a really beautifully written book . . . another page-turner.'

Nikki Thomas, Stressy Mummy Blog

jm-forster.com

This book is for you, dear reader.

Chapter One

"I've had an amazing week," Beth said to Jack, before taking a swig from her water bottle.

They were perched on a roof ridge, looking across to the other Victorian rooftops stretching into the distance. Jack glanced up and spotted a lonely jet trail, white against the afternoon sky. Beth spoke again, snapping his attention back to her. "The campsite was brilliant, by a stream, in the woods. We went to the beach and had barbecue kebabs every night. Pete told ghost stories that scared the others, especially Mia – not me though. I even picked up a tan!" She rolled up her sleeve to expose a forearm.

"Barely," said Jack, peering at her skin that was almost as pasty as his own. They'd had a freak heatwave over the October half term, to his disgust. It meant he'd been stuck in the flat – even when Dad had visited – hiding from the blistering sun that he was allergic to, praying *he* didn't end up looking like a burnt kebab.

As Beth chattered on about her holiday with her guardians, Jack switched his gaze back to the jumbled landscape of rooftops and twisted old chimneys. At least he'd been able to escape onto the tiles at sunset. The city roofs were his safe space, where he felt less like the weirdo with cream-coated, greasy skin. It was the one place he could really be himself, and practise his beloved game – jumping between shadows on the rooftops. One wrong move, and he'd be toast – but it kept his boredom at bay.

"Anyway," said Beth, nudging him and grinning. "It's more of a tan than I got spending the summer with you."

"True." Jack smiled back as he remembered meeting Beth for the first time on the roofs at twilight. "Met" was perhaps the wrong word – saved him when he slipped, more like. What did he think of her then, with her startling black and white make-up? That she looked like a vampire or a zombie? He didn't remember. Anyway, she'd come along at the perfect moment. Not only because she'd saved his life, but because she'd been there for him when everyone else had treated him as if he had the plague. She'd understood what it was like not to fit in.

"Here." Beth stood and pushed her hand into her jacket pocket and brought out a pinkish-grey cone-shaped shell. "Unusual, isn't it? Perfect for you. It's from Witcombe beach. You remember, it's where I used to go with Mum and Dad. Cathy and Pete knew I wanted to visit again, so . . ."

Jack took the shell and turned it over, running his fingers over its smooth curves. "Thanks. It's cool." A few grains of sand trickled into his palm.

"What about you?" she asked, giving him a searching look. "Did your dad come?"

He pocketed the shell and stared again across the Victorian slopes and chimney pots outlined against the reddening sun. "For a bit."

"Yeah? How did that go?" Although Jack and Beth had only met a few months ago, she knew how tricky things were with his dad. After Dad had done a disappearing act, he and Beth travelled together to find him, desperate for his help with Jack's worsening skin. He'd turned up in the end, thank goodness. Finding a cure for Jack's allergy was another thing altogether. Beth had been there to pick up the pieces when he'd discovered the truth.

"It was good. Too short though," he muttered. "He had to leave early to go back to Aberdeen."

"Shame. Still, you'll see him at Christmas, won't you?"

"Maybe. He was vague, as usual. Said something about problems getting time off work, Mum not wanting him around now they're separated. Blah, blah, blah." Dad had promised him that despite living in Scotland now, he'd keep in touch, but it wasn't turning out to be so simple. "Oh, I hung out with Fabien too."

"Sounds fun," said Beth. "See, I thought you'd be all right without me around."

And he had been all right. Fabien was a younger boy from school whom Jack had got to know recently. Hanging out and playing video games with him had been great – just not enough to fill the endless, sunny daylight hours. "Yeah, but Fabien's been in a strange mood all week. Guess what? He asked if I'd teach him how to shadow jump."

"You're kidding!" Beth chuckled. "What did you say?"

"As if. He'd be like a baby giraffe on ice," said Jack, shrugging. "No idea why he asked."

"You're his hero. He wants to be like you." She raised both hands, palms out, and did a bow of mock worship.

"Not likely." Jack's cheeks blazed with embarrassment and he adjusted his hood, to make sure it

4

protected his scalp from what remained of the sun's rays. "He's lonely. I get that."

"Yeah, I know . . . I'm sorry I had to go away," said Beth, not sounding sorry at all. "But Cathy and Pete are really into camping." She plucked at an imaginary thread on her sleeve. "I mean, I'd have loved to spend the week up here with you, but . . ." She trailed off, before adding, "Hey, I bet you didn't have time to miss me that much, with the new shadow jumping moves you've learnt." She bent to zip her bottle into her bag.

Jack shrugged. He realised Beth needed to spend time with Cathy and Pete, who'd become her guardians after the car crash which killed her mum and dad. They, Mia, who Beth shared a room with, and their other kids were her substitute family, after all. *But just how much fun did she have without me?*

"What's eating you?" Beth studied him. "You've been in a mood since I told you about going camping."

"I haven't," he said, frowning, although irritation itched at him like his sun-sensitive skin. It bugged Jack that she'd spent the half-term away. It bugged him more that she'd made all these friends at school. Like Sadie, who was in *all* her classes, and her tutor group too. Apart from Fabien, who wasn't even in their year, Jack didn't mix with anyone else. The reason . . . his stupid allergy. His sore, rash-prone skin made him stand out. And not

5

in a good way. It felt as if Beth was drifting away – that he was losing her to her new friends.

She stared at him. "Come on, 'fess up, or I'll have to make you."

"Okay, since you mention it . . ." But he stopped, not sure if he should carry on. She stood in front of him, hands on skinny hips, head tilted to the side in a question, her lips pinched together . . . Why shouldn't he tell her that she was abandoning him? He took a deep breath. "It's as if you don't want to hang out with me any more."

"What? Course I do. I've been busy, that's all. I'm here now, aren't I?" There was an edge to her voice.

"Yeah, right." An uneasy silence stretched between them. Jack squirted a blob of sun cream into his palm and rubbed it into his face and neck. As usual, his hair got in the way and received a sticky dollop too. He felt her eyes on him as he massaged the gloop into the tips of his ears. "My skin's frying," he said at last. "And we still have to finish fixing the zip wire."

"I'll do it. You can stay in the shade. I know what needs to be done."

He grunted.

"What . . . you're actually going to let me?" Beth said.

"Nope." Jack got to his feet, ramming the tube of cream in his trouser pocket, and pushed past her. "Just because you've done a few jumps with me doesn't mean you're a pro. Plus, remember what happened last time we tried this jump?"

"It was raining then," she said. "And we were being chased by that blockhead."

She was talking about Kai. It had been a dangerous move, getting on the wrong side of the older boy they'd encountered when they'd trespassed on his roof terrace. It had led to loads of trouble. They were both silent for a moment, the memories of the summer still vivid. "All the same, I'd better do the jump."

"Oh . . . okay," she said, hurt in her voice.

He felt a guilty pang. But she could hardly expect him to let her do the risky stuff when she was so out of practice.

"Stay here," he ordered, rotating his shoulders to relax the muscles, then jiggling his arms and legs to loosen them.

"Yes, sir, I won't move a muscle. Promise."

Chapter Two

Jack took a couple of deep breaths to calm himself, then broke into a run, somersaulting and leaping from one shadow to the next, as he made his way up inclines and down slopes. Each sequence of moves had its challenges. But he was well-practised. Twist this way, swing that. Jump. Land on the toes and ball of one foot, then the other. Lean, aim shoulder to the ground and roll. Bounce up. Check balance. Run to wall, push off with feet and twist, land with bended knees. Perfect. Move on.

Once he'd reached a prominent ridge, Jack stopped and took in his surroundings. The fiery end-of-day October sun spilt between the Victorian chimney stacks, splattering patches of golden light on the red tiles. In the distance he glimpsed the cathedral's brickwork glinting in the late afternoon light. He inhaled the cool air, savouring the moment before the sun disappeared. This roof was hidden amongst a warren of steep pitches, one slope leading to another, criss-crossing the old part of the city like a giant maze above the streets. Not a problem for him, though – he knew the rooftops like the back of his hand.

His gaze swooped to the alleyway far below, taking in the line of wheelie bins used by the high street shops and the stacks of crushed cardboard boxes beside them. Traffic whooshed past the mouth of the alley in a steady stream, but on the roof the noise of the cars was muffled by distance and the caws of the gulls. His mind flashed back again to when he and Beth had been on that particular rooftop. He remembered how they'd fled Kai by leaping across the chasm to the other side. How Beth had fallen. How he'd saved her, but in the process spilt her parents' ashes that she carried in her backpack. She definitely hadn't planned to scatter them on the drenched tiles. That had been a low point in their friendship. But they had got over it and were still friends. Weren't they?

He glanced at the nylon rope coiled on the tiles beside him. One end trailed up to the stout chimney stack on the ridge behind, where earlier he'd knotted it around the solid bricks. He picked up the coil, looping it across his neck and over one shoulder. It felt reassuringly strong.

He breathed in . . . then out, calming his body and mind.

One, two, three, four, five paces . . .

Jack bounded into the air, eyes focused on the roof across the void. For half a moment he thought he wouldn't make it, that the jump was too far. But he landed without a hitch: knees bent, balanced on the toes and balls of his feet, trainers gripping the tiles, his heart hopping in his throat and adrenaline pumping through him. He gave himself a minute to relax, then scuttled up the pitch towards a thick steel vent pipe jutting from the top of the roof. He'd left a bag tucked at the base of the pipe the other day with the rest of the equipment he needed. First, though, he had to tie the rope.

With both hands grasping the pipe, he twisted his legs around and shimmied upwards. Two rims, ten centimetres apart, jutted out, forming chunky rings around the metal. Jack wound the rope between them, pulling it taut and securing it with tight knots he'd learnt online. After he'd slid down again, he opened the bag, pulled out a steel handle bar and clipped it onto the rope. He stood back with a satisfied grin to study his handiwork. It was perfect.

The rope formed a makeshift zip wire over the alleyway. Jack's idea for extra fun, but it had a more serious use too: a shortcut between the roofs, an escape route should they need it. And who knew when that might be? Jack shuddered at the memory of Kai's leering face as he'd booted Jack in the ribs three months ago, on these very rooftops. For some reason that Jack still didn't understand, Kai had taken an instant dislike to him and Beth – furious, maybe, that they'd invaded his space. As if Kai had something to hide. Jack didn't have a clue what that would be. Well, it didn't matter. A bully, that was what Kai was, and a thug. Jack snorted and kicked a hefty piece of moss with the toe of his trainer. It skittered down the slates and tipped off the edge of the roof.

"Done?"

Jack turned. Beth was standing behind him. "What . . . You jumped . . ." For a second Jack couldn't get the words out. "I told you to stay put. You could have been killed!"

"But I wasn't," she said, her dark eyes flashing. "And I'm fine – it was fine."

Next time, listen to me, he wanted to say, but that made him sound like Mum. Plus, Beth didn't like being told what to do. Instead, he tugged on the zip wire again. "It'll work better when I've got proper wire and a pulley system, but I'll have to save my allowance for that."

"Can I test it? Before it's too dark."

He was cross with Beth for taking risks, and he felt like saying no, but it was getting late, and he wasn't in the mood for a fight. So he stepped to one side, stuffing his hands in his pockets, as he watched her take the handle and ready herself. The wire ran steeply

11

downwards, across the gap between the buildings, levelling out on the lower roof towards the end of the run. Enough space to slow to a gradual stop. He hoped.

She took a running jump and launched herself off the rooftop. Jack couldn't help grinning at Beth's excited whooping as she sped along the cable, her long, skinny legs stretched out in front, jet-black hair flowing behind her. He unhitched the belt of his trousers, threw it over the wire as a crude handle and followed. Despite his doubts, the belt worked well, and as he picked up speed, the breeze whipped his hood back to expose his scalp to the cool air. The city crematorium flashed into view, with its stones set into the earth like giant grey teeth, then vanished behind a building.

"What a rush," said Beth, as Jack landed, planting his feet on the tiles next to hers.

He grinned again, suddenly in a better mood. Being on the rooftops always helped. He sprang into his planned sequence of shadow jumping moves – bouncing off the brickwork, spinning and twisting in mid-air to reach the next bit of shade, swinging under metal railings bordering the different rooftops, leapfrogging over low walls, his arms propelling him forwards. He was conscious of nothing but his next move, his steady, controlled breathing, and the rhythmic thud of his heart.

One final somersault and he skidded to a halt on the peak of a roof they didn't often use.

Moments later Beth joined him, panting hard. "Cool view." She cupped her hand over her eyes. "Hey, what's that?" Jack squinted to where she pointed. Something black was wedged between the rickety chimney pots on the next rooftop.

"Let's check it out," he said, and headed up that way.

It turned out to be a plastic bin liner, damp and cold to Jack's touch. There was something solid inside. To escape the icy gusts of wind, they sat against a stack and Jack pulled open the bag. Inside was a large, brown, padded postal envelope, the same size as an A3 sheet of paper but as thick as a school textbook. Jack prodded it – it felt squidgy and dense. Whoever had sealed the flap with brown parcel tape hadn't done a good job as the tape was peeling away at the edges.

"Say it's a bomb?" he said, holding the packet at arms' length. "Perhaps we'd better leave it." He was half-joking, but he'd never found anything on the rooftops before. For all they knew, it *could* be a bomb.

Beth arched an eyebrow at him. "Aren't you tempted to look?"

He shrugged. Part of him thought they should shove it back where they'd found it. Messing with this might end in trouble. And what with his manic search to find

Dad and a cure for his worsening sun allergy, he'd had his fair share of that over the last few months. But before he had the chance to decide what to do with the packet, Beth reached over and snatched it from him. "If you're not going to look, I will."

"Hey! Give it back," he said with a flash of annoyance.

"Too late!" She twisted away from him, holding the packet aloft in her left hand as she ripped the tape with her right. "I'm dying to find out what it is . . .'

Chapter Three

Bundles of ten, twenty and fifty-pound notes spilled into Beth's palms and onto her lap.

Jack whistled, his irritation forgotten. "That's one giant wad of cash!"

"There must be thousands here," Beth said.

Jack grabbed a handful of the notes and flicked them with his thumb. "Think anyone would miss it if we . . . ?"

"You're kidding, right?" Beth gave him a withering look. "Don't even go there."

Jack yanked his hood further over his head. "I wasn't being serious. Why on earth is there a load of money up here? A drugs deal?"

"Wait, something's written on the envelope," Beth said, and Jack followed her gaze. She was right. Something was scribbled in faded, smudged blue ink on the dirty address label.

Beth gave a tiny gasp. "This envelope is from The Willows!"

"The Willows?"

"Yeah, you know, the place where we've been volunteering for the past two months, and where Fabien's grandad lives?" She quirked an eyebrow at him.

Jack scowled at her. "But why's an envelope from there up here?" He scanned the area, soon making out the distinctive domed glass roof of The Willows retirement home lit up against the sky.

Beth nibbled her top lip. "I bet some of the people at The Willows keep cash under the mattress. My nan used to do it. She thought it was safer than a bank."

"But why dump the money up here?"

"It's not as if it's *really* been dumped." She thrust the notes back in the envelope and attempted to stick it down with the now un-sticky parcel tape. "Maybe it *is* drug money."

"Let's forget about it. Or better, hand it in to the police."

"Really?" said Beth. "How are you going to explain what we were doing on the roofs?"

She had a point. It would put an end to shadow jumping for sure. "We don't have to say where we found it."

"What are you gonna say? You're a terrible liar, Jack. They'd get it out of you. Then they'll think we stole it. Anyway, don't you want to find out who picks it up?"

"You mean hang around for some drug dealer to show up? Er . . ." Jack put a finger on his chin, pretending to consider the question. "No." He grabbed the packet and stood up. An extra strong squall of wind caught Jack off balance. He stumbled, and the packet slipped from his hands and skittered down the slope. The flap came loose and they both watched in horror as bank notes cascaded from the envelope, fluttering and swirling on the tiles.

Jack and Beth careered down the slope, leaping and springing into the air to catch the flying notes. A few escaped and spun in the breeze, to end up who knew where. As Jack scooped a handful up from the gutter, something flickered in the corner of his eye. Someone was on a neighbouring roof ridge, their dark shape silhouetted against the sunset sky. The figure turned and Jack swallowed a gasp. It was Kai. A familiar icy dread spread through Jack's guts. They hadn't seen Kai since the summer, and Jack hoped that he'd grown bored of the rooftops. But there he was, as large and as menacing as ever. If Kai glanced to his right, he'd spot them and the remaining notes swirling in the breeze.

He grabbed Beth's arm and pulled her down onto the tiles, then picked up a broken bit of tile and lobbed it hard over the ridge. There was a faint clattering as it landed somewhere away to their left. Jack craned his neck to see what was happening. Kai paused, then, like a sniffer dog following a scent, made off towards the noise. Jack and Beth wasted no time in scurrying around, picking up what remaining notes they could find and stuffing them into the envelope.

"Here," panted Beth. She pushed the packet into Jack's hands. He sealed the envelope as best he could, hurtled up the incline to the chimneys, shoved the envelope in the black bag and crammed it between the pots. He slipped back down the roof to Beth and they flattened themselves against the tiles once more.

After a minute's wait, Jack dared to peek over the ridge and saw Kai crouching by the chimneys where the packet was. Jack ducked down once again.

"Should have known it would be something to do with *him*," he said to Beth in an angry whisper. The older boy was the only other person Jack had ever seen on the roofs. "What on earth's he doing with a load of money?"

"Lowlife," muttered Beth.

Jack weighed up their options for escape, in case they had to flee. To the left was a sheer drop at the edge of the building. The other way led to a tricky combination of shadow jumps, and with the sun almost set, it would be suicide to contemplate that. The newly completed zip wire was not far, but Kai stood between them and it. Beth shifted, sending a piece of loose debris rattling down the tiles. They both froze, listening, Beth squeezing her eyes shut, as if that would stop whatever came next from happening. Jack's heart pounded in his mouth.

Finally, after not hearing the smallest sound apart from the birds calling overhead, they crawled up the roof and peered over the ridge. Kai and the packet were gone.

Jack collapsed back onto the tiles, the adrenaline leaving his body as fast as the air from a popped balloon. The events of the last few minutes replayed in his head as he took a moment to catch his breath. Despite the danger, he'd got a real kick from it. Beth must have felt it too.

"You remember before when Kai chased us and . . ." he started.

Beth's phone beeped insistently and, immediately distracted, she swiped through her messages. "Gotta go. Catch you tomorrow, yeah?"

Jack felt a stab of disappointment as Beth got to her feet and started picking her way up the roof. *Doesn't she want to talk about what just happened?* She turned when she reached the ridge, calling, "Oh, what were you saying?"

"Doesn't matter." The moment for telling her it was "like old times" had passed.

She shrugged. "See ya then."

He watched as she disappeared over the ridge, then reappeared on the next rooftop, getting smaller and smaller until finally she vanished.

Chapter Four

At school the next morning Jack had zero chance to talk to Beth about what had happened on the rooftops. He couldn't get her on her own, for one thing – Sadie stuck to her side like a limpet. Maths, science and French passed in a blur, as questions and doubts rattled in his head, the big one being: what were they going to do about Kai and the packet of money?

At lunchtime, Jack went to the library. Not that it was his favourite place or anything, but having skin that fried in the sun quicker than bacon in a pan meant he had to spend break and lunchtimes inside, sometimes on his own – ever since Beth had been busy with Sadie, and her other new mates – and sometimes with Fabien. Jack and Fabien had first met in the library at the start of term – Jack driven there by the sun, the younger boy by a lack of friends. It didn't matter that Fabien was in the year below Jack – they got on well. Jack understood what it was like to be lonely. He'd been there, done that. Just as the rooftops were Jack's safe space, the library and books had become Fabien's. If Jack could have made Fabien's life at school one iota better for him, he would have done it.

Today Fabien was perched in his usual spot, on top of the radiator between the history reference shelf and fiction A to D. He had one of his favourite books in his hand – the one where super-brainy spiders invade the world and take revenge on the spider-killing humans. Fabien's dream was to become a film director or screenwriter, he'd told Jack. Except he hadn't actually written any stories down yet, despite having loads to tell. Jack reckoned Fabien should start making videos and putting them online. Fabien lived with . . . what was it that Mum called it? Oh, yeah, his head in the clouds.

As if to prove what a daydreamer he was, Fabien wasn't actually reading the book in his hands, but staring into the distance, a faraway look on his face.

"Hey." Jack nudged Fabien's leg away to grab a spot for himself on the lukewarm pipes.

"Hi," muttered Fabien, at last registering Jack's arrival. He lowered the book and scrubbed at his eyes.

"Here." Jack rummaged in his backpack and brought out a green woollen beanie hat. "You left this at mine the other day."

"Great, thanks!" Fabien balanced his book next to him on the radiator and took the hat, looking pleased. "I thought I'd lost it when . . ." He broke off.

"When what?" asked Jack. Fabien's grandad had given Fabien the beanie hat. He always wore it when not at school, *always*. So how come he'd forgotten it at Jack's place?

"Doesn't matter." Fabien was suddenly busy stuffing the hat in his school bag.

"You look like death," said Jack. Fabien's uniform was creased and dirty, as if he'd been sleeping under one of the railway arches down the road, and his mass of sand-coloured hair was even messier than normal. Jack thought the boy had turned prickly in the last couple of weeks, and so far no amount of coaxing and probing had made him open up about what was on his mind. He wondered if it had something to do with Harry and Sam, Fabien's so-called friends – every time Jack asked, Fabien clammed up.

"Thanks," Fabien said again, and stifled a yawn. "I didn't sleep last night."

Jack studied his face, plastered with freckles and worry lines. "What's wrong?"

"Nothing." Fabien's voice wobbled though. Then he scrubbed at his hair. "I'm just tired. And I've got double maths this afternoon with Boring Burton. I'm gonna die."

Jack grinned, relieved to hear Fabien talking more like his normal self. "You want me to sit in your class and keep pinching you?"

"I don't think even that would work today. I'm going to need an electric shock to keep me awake. *And* I bet Boring Burton gives us loads of homework." This time Fabien didn't try to hide his yawn. "Hey, Dad bought me the new MegaSpy game. It's really cool."

"Lucky you. Can I have a go sometime?"

"I'll lend it to you . . . if you teach me how to shadow jump . . ."

"That again?" said Jack, rolling his eyes. "Why the sudden obsession with shadow jumping? It's not easy, you know."

Fabien shrugged. "I just want to learn. I've watched some videos about parkour."

"Have you?" Jack was surprised. Fabien actually seemed serious!

"Yeah. You're always talking about it. It sounds cool."

"I'll think about it." Jack tried but failed to picture Fabien performing somersaults on the rooftops with him and Beth.

Fabien glanced out of the nearby window and gave an enormous sigh which shook his skinny frame. "Sam and Harry have gone off together again."

"Ah, right." Jack knew how *that* felt – being dumped by people you thought were your friends had happened to him more times than he could remember. Fabien had told Jack that Sam and Harry had been his mates since primary school, but it seemed it was true what they said about three being a crowd. It so happened that Fabien was number three.

"You're too loyal to them," said Jack. "They're not your real friends if they treat you like that. And friends would help you when you had a problem. Would Sam or Harry do that?"

"I'd do it for *them*." Fabien focused his red-rimmed eyes on Jack. *Has he been crying?* wondered Jack.

"Anyway, they're not that bad," said Fabien, picking his book back up. "They hang out with me sometimes."

"Yeah, when it suits them. Look, they're not the only people in year nine. You should ditch them and find other friends," said Jack, although he of all people knew how tricky *that* was.

"It's not that easy."

"Good job I'm around then, isn't it?" he joked, but this time Fabien didn't even raise a smile. "Things seem bad right now, but they will get better, I promise. Take it from someone who knows."

"It's not that . . ." Fabien trailed off.

"What is it then?" Jack jumped in. "Your grandad? Is he okay?"

"Why wouldn't he be?" squeaked Fabien, panic flashing across his face.

"Hey, cool it," said Jack, alarmed. "I was only asking. When are you visiting again? Next week?"

Fabien thrummed his heels against the radiator pipes, earning him a tut from a passing sixth form prefect. He stopped until she'd disappeared, then started up again. "Tomorrow."

"So soon?" Jack stared at him. Something was definitely up. Although close to his grandad, Fabien never used to visit Mr Garibaldi at The Willows more than once or twice a week; now it was turning into nearly every day.

"Yeah." Fabien buried his gaze in the carpet and didn't offer an explanation.

"What about Bertie?" probed Jack. Bertie was Fabien's black and white terrier. Fabien was always going on about him. One day he'd even brought Bertie with him when he'd come to hang out at Jack's place.

The bond between the two of them had been obvious. "Don't you usually walk him after school?"

"I can do both things."

Unease rippled through Jack. He'd spent loads of time with Fabien's grandad over the last few weeks, chatting over tea and crumbly homemade biscuits in the lounge. Say there was something Mr Garibaldi wasn't telling him? Maybe it wasn't Fabien who had the problem, but the old man . . . "Is your grandad sick?"

"I told you," said Fabien. "He's fine."

Fabien wasn't going to open up, that was clear. Jack shifted position on the radiator. He would have to wait until Fabien chose to talk. Time to cheer him up with his story of Kai and the packet of cash.

"You'll never guess what happened on the roofs—"

Fabien jumped off his radiator perch, the book falling from his hands. "Catch you later."

"Hey, where are you going?" said Jack.

"To buy some lunch." Fabien mumbled.

"It's pasta today. You hate pasta—" But Fabien had ducked away between the bookcases, leaving Jack to pick up the book and put it back on the shelf.

Chapter Five

I'll be late, Beth's message read. Nothing else. No explanation. No smiley face. Nothing. Jack sighed as he pocketed his phone and trailed down the tree-lined street after school. Beth was probably hanging out with Sadie again.

Halfway along the road, the narrow, tightly packed red-brick houses gave way to larger buildings, some of which had been converted into flats. Jack stopped outside a massive house set back from the others. "The Willows Retirement Apartments" read the sign at the entrance. It was a grand Victorian building with long windows surrounded by fancy brickwork and steep roofs. The mass of pitches and twisted chimneys hid the striking glass dome from the street. A set of steps and a ramp led up to the main doors. What must have once been a thin strip of garden was mostly tarmacked over for parking, but on one side stood a small fountain with two carved stone fish leaping out of the water. As Jack stared up at the imposing building, his thoughts flashed back to the conversation he'd had with Beth on the roofs a month ago, when she'd first suggested volunteering at the home.

"Cathy knows Malcolm, one of the managers," Beth had said. "He's always in need of help, and he said I could play their piano for the residents. You'll volunteer too, won't you? It'll be fun."

Hanging out in a care home with a load of old people wasn't Jack's idea of fun, he remembered telling her.

"It's not a care home," explained Beth. "It's like a tiny village for retired people. They all have their own apartments. And other communal rooms to use if they want. They've even got a cinema."

Actually, Jack had started enjoying his visits, especially since he'd met Mr Garibaldi, he thought as he mounted the steps to the main doors and pushed them open. The entrance lobby was one of those places that screamed, "Look, but don't touch!' It was stuffed full of polished, expensive-looking furniture, and had a glistening chandelier dangling from the ceiling. The lobby led to an airy hall with a reception desk and little office. Signposts in the shape of fingers pointed the way to the restaurant, lounge, cinema, library and other rooms that the residents shared. An iron-work double staircase curled left and right of the reception desk, up to the galleried first and second floors and the residents' apartments.

High above Jack's head was the impressive glass dome he saw from the rooftops. Strips of black metal separated the pieces of glass, making it look like a giant spider's web. He stopped to stare up at the sky, tinged an orange-yellow by the lights of the city. A sliver of moon appeared and disappeared again as feathery clouds slid across its pale surface. He'd seen this dome many times from above, but from below it was something else. Despite his awe, he couldn't help imagining blazing light cascading into the building during the day, flooding the stairwell, bouncing off the black-and-white floor tiles and shiny furniture. He shuddered, glad the sun was just about to set, and he didn't have to worry about his skin blistering. Even reflected light was a danger to him.

He turned his attention to the reception desk and checked the cubbyhole office next to it. No sign of the managers, Malcolm and Nina. Jack exhaled softly, relieved. Nina always found something to moan about. He fished his volunteer pass out of his pocket and looped it around his neck, as usual trying not to mind the photo, which made him look like someone had kicked him up the backside. Nina had taken it before he'd had the chance to pose properly for the camera. His only consolation was that Beth's photo was just as bad.

Ray, the cleaner, was hoovering in the corridor. Jack skipped over the power cable snaking across the floor, waving a hand at the cleaner as he went by, and entered the lounge. Little groups of squishy armchairs dotted the room, and the longest sofa he'd ever seen sat in front of the enormous stone fireplace. A fire crackled in the hearth, even though the room was so stuffy he could hardly breathe.

Four women sat reading newspapers or looking out through the patio windows onto the darkening garden. They each looked about a hundred years old. Another group was at a small table playing cards. A trolley piled with plates, cakes and cutlery stood in the middle of the room, and Conchita, one of the catering assistants, was busy slopping tea into cups.

"Hello, Jack. Mr Garibaldi's been waiting for you." Conchita beamed, the lines on her leathery face deepening, and gestured towards the sofa. "You can give him some cake."

Jack took a cup and saucer and plate, and hurried to the sofa where Fabien's grandad was sitting on his own. Mr G was not only Fabien's grandad but Jack's favourite person at The Willows. They'd hit it off straight away, and Mr Garibaldi made a point of being in the lounge when he knew Jack was coming. Jack's own grandparents were dead, but Mr Garibaldi was like a grandfather to him.

Jack's mum would have described Mr Garibaldi as "a proper gent". Today he was wearing a murky green jacket and cords. Under the jacket Jack glimpsed a woollen waistcoat and a stripy brown tie with a faint stain. Long strands of wispy white hair had strayed from a hair-tie and framed his pale cheeks. Although he'd shaved, there were tufts of stubble sprouting here and there on his chin, as if he wasn't up to finishing the job.

Jack placed the cup on the low table in front of Mr G and handed him the plate. Mr G started tucking into the jam sponge cake straight away.

"How's things?" Jack sat down in the armchair next to the sofa.

Mr Garibaldi coughed as he swallowed a mouthful of cake, crumbs flying from between his lips. "Can't complain, lad, can't complain," he said once he'd recovered. He looked at Jack through watery grey eyes, magnified behind thick-rimmed glasses. "Though the leg's giving me a bit of grief." As Mr Garibaldi shifted, his trousers slid up slightly, revealing something black and shiny where his shin should have been. Jack averted his gaze, not wanting Mr G to catch him staring. He'd never asked why the old man had an artificial limb, worried that it would appear rude. But since Mr G had mentioned it . . .

'What happened to your leg?' he asked.

"Lost it in the war," said Mr Garibaldi, breaking off his cake-eating to pull his trouser leg up further and rap the exposed shin with his knuckles.

"The *Second* World War?" said Jack.

Mr Garibaldi gave a chuckle. "Certainly not the First. Even if I look that old."

"Were you in the army?"

"Oh no, I was only three when the war broke out. Always been a good runner, I have, even in those days." He puffed his chest out. "But I couldn't outrun a bomb. Got hit on the way to the air raid shelter in our garden. The bomb landed on the house next door. Luckily, our neighbours weren't at home when it hit."

"What about your family?"

"All survived unharmed," he said. "Thank goodness."

They both sat quietly. Jack was imagining what he'd do if he only had one and a half real legs. How would he shadow jump?

"Pass my tea, there's a good lad," said Mr G after a few minutes.

Jack leant forwards and picked up the cup. A little card had got stuck to the bottom of the saucer. He peeled it away, glancing at it. "Write a Will with Bill!" was stamped in gold lettering across the centre of the card, with a phone number and other contact details underneath. More of the cards were strewn across the coffee table.

Conchita stopped next to the sofa with her trolley to pick up some dirty cups and started tidying the cards into a pile. "Bill Slide's been coming here for years," she explained to Jack as he examined the card. "Some people need help with legal stuff."

"Sharks," said Mr Garibaldi. "The lot of them."

"Careful what you say, Albert. Bill's a good friend of Nina." Conchita gave him a gentle smile.

Mr Garibaldi looked thoughtful as Conchita trundled off, before turning his attention back to Jack. "So, what news have you got for me, young Jack? How did the half-term break go with your dad?"

"It was great, but he had to leave early cos of work."

Mr G gazed at him. "That's a real shame."

"Yeah." Jack realised that he'd scrunched the business card in his fist.

"And Beth was busy with her folks, I suppose."

Jack nodded. Mr G had a knack of knowing what he was feeling without him saying anything at all.

"You must be very proud to have a dad like him."

"Yeah." Jack was proud of him, it was true. Dad had been one of the best scientists in his field when he was younger – he'd even won awards for his work. But false rumours about his dad carrying out experiments on children at Bioscience Discoveries, the labs where he'd worked, had put an end to his ground-breaking research into anti-ageing drugs. It had broken Jack's dad for a long while – years in fact. Jack remembered all the temporary jobs Dad had taken, all the house moves, the changes of school for him, the arguments between Mum and Dad, them splitting up, Dad disappearing for a while . . . Dad's new job in Aberdeen was his chance for a fresh start.

"Tough for you," continued Mr G after a pause. "Only seeing your dad in the holidays and the odd weekend."

Jack nodded, swallowing the lump that had formed in his throat. Dad's love of his work and the distance to Aberdeen meant Jack didn't see him as much as he'd like. And he always had the feeling that Dad might disappear again. That he'd forget about Jack. Mr G seemed to understand all that.

"I saw Fabien a bit too over half-term," Jack said, at last finding his voice.

The old man's eyes lit up on hearing his grandson's name. "Ah, good, good." He sat quietly for a moment, then placed his cup and plate carefully back on the table with a sigh. "I don't know what's got into Fabien lately, but he's not right. Something's bothering him. Has he said anything to you?"

Jack shook his head. So he wasn't the only one to notice the change in Fabien. "I've asked, but Fabien won't tell me. I'll keep trying."

Mr Garibaldi sank back into the sofa cushions again. "Thanks, lad. I'm sure you'll get to the bottom of it—" A thunderous crash of piano notes cut Mr G off. Beth had arrived. She was at the grand piano at the far end of the room, her back and shoulders hunched in concentration as her fingers stumbled over the keys. The sound was like a thousand plates being dropped, again and again and again. The tune was something classical, vaguely familiar. As far as Jack could tell, Beth was murdering it.

With the fingertips of each hand pressed gently together, Mr G tipped his head back and closed his eyes. "Pure talent."

Chapter Six

Malcolm and Nina were too busy arguing behind the reception desk to notice Jack and Beth approaching on their way out. Nina's cropped black hair bobbed backwards and forwards in time to the finger jabs she aimed at Malcolm's podgy chest. Jack exchanged glances with Beth and they slowed down, curious to find out what was going on. Beth bent as if to tie the lace of her trainer, while Jack pretended to examine a rack of sales leaflets positioned close to the desk.

"We need more cameras, more surveillance . . ." Nina was saying. As Jack peeked round the leaflet rack, he noticed Nina's large white front teeth were smeared with lipstick, as if they'd been splashed with blood.

"We've already got keypads at the entrances, and a security guard, love," Malcolm replied. "It's been months since we installed the cameras and Jolly hasn't picked up anything suspicious. We don't have the money—"

"I've told Jolly to do spot checks on the staff."

Malcolm's eyes widened. Jack could almost feel his alarm at Nina's words. "They won't like it, love."

"Dr Bellini has already reported the theft to the police so he can claim on his insurance."

"There you go – the matter is dealt with." Malcolm's bald spot glistened under the bright lights above the desk. "I don't see that we need to do any more."

"Don't be ridiculous. It's typical of you to bury your head in the sand," said Nina. "Dr Bellini's not the only one. The Johnsons' bird ornament vanished, Mrs Joyliffe says she's lost a ring, and there's Henry's missing cash too. Word will get out. You know what people are like. We need to do something. Our reputation is at stake."

"That's why it's best to keep it quiet. Having the police around too much is bad publicity." Malcolm fingered the collar of his shirt, his fingers trembling slightly. "What do you propose I do, love?"

"Pressurise the police to investigate, otherwise we'll be out of business before the end of the year."

"Ah, Jack, hello." Malcolm's sweaty cheeks went as crimson as his nose as he finally noticed him standing there. "And Beth." Beth straightened up. "Nina, love,

38

let's not talk about this now. Leave it all to me. I'll handle it."

Nina shot Jack and Beth a none-too-friendly glare before saying to Malcolm, "Make sure you *do* handle it. We don't want any *undesirables* in here, do we?" She punctuated each word with a slap of the desk, then plonked her backside on the chair in front of the ancient computer. Nina fired an abrupt, "Haven't you two got homes to go to?", turned her back on them and started tapping furiously at the keyboard.

"You know what this means, don't you?" said Beth, as they left the main entrance and hurried through the car park.

Jack's mind was blank. "Er, no?"

"Henry's money must be the cash we found on the roof. There's a thief at The Willows. It's our new case, Dr Watson. You up for it?" Beth's phone started ringing and she glanced at the screen.

"Er . . . sure," Jack replied.

"Great!" Beth bounded off, phone clamped to her ear, leaving Jack staring after her.

She wanted to play detectives. Again. She was being impulsive. Again.

She was off to hang out with Sadie. Again.

*

When Jack got home from The Willows, his mum was in the sitting room. She was in full-on manic mode, bundling yet more clothes into an already bulging suitcase open on the floor. "Auntie Lil will be here later. She's got the spare key."

"Okay," he mumbled, stifling a massive yawn. He watched as Mum squashed the contents down to close the lid. "What's happening?"

"I told you yesterday. I've got a work trip to Tamchester." Mum sat back on her heels and studied him. "I knew you weren't listening."

"I just forgot."

Mum zipped the suitcase, stood up and gave him another of her probing looks. "Bad day?"

He made a face. She knew school wasn't his favourite place. There was no denying that his sun allergy made it difficult for him to fit in. Beth *had* made things tons better. But now she had Sadie to hang out with at school and was spending more time with her family too . . .

"Jack?" Mum prompted him, pushing her greying hair from her temples. "You've got that sucking-a-lemon look again. Problem?"

"No, no problem." He followed her as she wheeled her suitcase into the hallway.

"Good," said Mum, distracted, the car keys jangling in her hand. "There's a cake in the tin to tide you over till dinner. I'm only a phone call away if you need me. And ten days is not that long."

"I'll be fine."

Jack faked a grin, hoping that would satisfy her. Mum had a super-sensitive radar that honed in on the slightest change in his mood. It had become especially acute since she and Dad had split up. However hard he tried to reassure her that he was okay, it was never enough. If he came back from school one day and wanted to be on his own listening to music, she'd be banging on his bedroom door within seconds, wondering if he was all right. He was sure she'd only bought him a new phone after his got broken so that she could keep tabs on him. Jack wished she would stop treating him like a three-year-old. At fourteen, he was old enough to take care of himself. But at least Mum hadn't asked Mrs Roberts from the flat opposite to look after him. He *hated* that. She was so nosey. Auntie Lil, on the other hand, let Jack do his own thing most of the time. She lived near Bioscience Discoveries, and hadn't had a clue about half of the stuff he and Beth had got up to when they'd been looking for Dad. Yeah, Mum's going away was a good thing. He needed space.

"Be good," said Mum.

He followed her out of the flat and watched her roll the suitcase down the corridor into the lift. She waved as the doors swished shut. As he turned to go back inside, he noticed the door to Mrs Roberts's place opposite was ajar. She was standing in her hallway, her back towards him. She was muttering into her phone, her free arm alternating between cartwheeling and jabbing the air. Something had got his elderly neighbour fired up.

Mrs Roberts swung round and her eyes widened as she clocked him. She said a loud "bye" into the phone, then dropped it on a nearby table. She shuffled over to the door and pulled it wide open, peering past Jack and down the corridor towards the lift and stairwell. Her shabby dressing gown flapped open, revealing a pair of multi-coloured pyjama bottoms and a red top printed with the surprising words: "Hot stuff".

Mrs Roberts glanced at him again, before bundling the sides of the gown together and wrapping the belt tightly around her waist. "Hello?" She said it like a question.

"Hi, I was just saying bye—"

Mrs Roberts's phone buzzed loudly from the table, interrupting Jack. They both stared at it. She didn't move.

"Er, your phone's . . ." said Jack.

"Nuisance call," she said, fluttering a hand in the direction of the mobile, but making no effort to pick it up. "I get so many these days. Did you want to speak to me?"

Heat prickled across his cheeks. "No."

"Right, well, I'd better . . ." Mrs Roberts backed into her flat and shut the door, the knocker rattling against its plate.

There was a ping from the lift and the doors slid open, revealing a tall man in a sharp black suit and stripy tie, with thick salt-and-pepper hair greased back from his forehead. He stepped out of the lift and stopped, looking around. His sausage-like fingers gripped a shiny leather laptop bag.

He spotted Jack. "Hey, sonny, I'm looking for number seven."

"Mrs Roberts?" said Jack, startled. He'd never seen *anyone* visiting his elderly neighbour before.

"That's right, Mrs Roberts." The man gave Jack a slippery smile, revealing a row of impossibly white teeth. Jack pointed to her door, not saying anything.

"Thanks, sonny." The man strode up and knocked. Within seconds the door flew open and he was marshalled inside, leaving an over-powering pong of aftershave in his wake.

Chapter Seven

The cathedral bells chimed 4.30 p.m. From his vantage point on the roof, Jack watched the street lights flicker on. There was a chilly wind. Powerful gusts buffeted him from all sides, the sharp air slicing across his scalp. He glanced up at the overcast sky and shivered.

Meet me on the roofs after school! Stake-out time! Beth's message had read that morning. He'd replied with a thumbs up, although this hadn't been at the top of his list of things to do that afternoon. He'd planned to practise a few new moves he'd seen on a freerunning video, not stake out the chimney pots. But part of him was curious, and it was a chance to be with Beth. That made the decision a no-brainer.

What was keeping her? He'd give her another five minutes and head home – his insides were clawing with hunger. Auntie Lil would be making something tasty for dinner, and he didn't want to miss it.

A piece of broken tile bounced down the slope closest to him. "Finally!" he said, as Beth jumped to his side. "Where were you?"

"Sorry, I was with Sadie. She wanted to tell me something."

Sadie. The mention of her name made Jack's itchy skin prickle. "What did she want to tell you?"

Beth looked at him, frowning. "Nothing important."

"Maybe you should have got *her* to join you up here, since you've become so matey."

Beth's eyes widened and she placed her hands on her hips. "What's that supposed to mean?"

"Nothing," he muttered, cheeks flaming under her sharp gaze. He was being grumpy and unfair, but the thought of Beth moving on with her life, making new friends, while he stagnated like water in a smelly pond, was not the greatest feeling.

Jack set off, aware of Beth following. After two short sprints, a vault over metal railings and a twist with expert landing, they neared their lookout point. He slowed to allow his racing heart to recover and a flicker of movement caught his attention. Below and to their right, a skylight opened in a pitched roof. Jack pulled Beth down onto the tiles, placing a finger to his lips, and they peeked over the ridge. Beth shifted beside him as they stared at the familiar head with beanie hat which had appeared at the window. Jack's brain refused to believe what his eyes were telling him.

"It can't be," breathed Beth, obviously struggling with this sight too. "What's Fabien doing up here?"

They watched in silence as the younger boy poked a thin arm out and dropped a packet onto the roof. Then he slipped his slender body through the gap, snatched the packet up and, with another quick glance around, stumbled away.

Beth was the first to recover. She jumped to her feet and glanced at Jack. "Come on, he'll get hurt."

Jack jerked his hood over further to cover his scalp, his mind still buzzing from shock. A hundred questions jostled for his attention. What was Fabien doing up there? Why did he have a packet? What had he got himself involved in? Was he a thief? Jack swallowed a wave of fear for the boy, as he and Beth edged along the ridge until they were directly opposite the skylight. Fabien was tottering across the tiles towards a steep incline. His body wobbled like a puppet's, his jelly legs going in all directions at once. One hand hovered to the side to steady himself, the other clutched a packet similar to the one Jack and Beth had found a couple of days ago.

Jack's body tensed. The little hairs on his arms were standing on end. "He's gonna get himself killed."

He must have said it louder than he meant because Fabien whipped round. His eyes widened when he clocked them. But instead of stopping, Fabien tried to scuttle faster up the slope, his feet slipping and sliding on the tiles.

"Wait!" shouted Jack, his voice cracking. Time to move. With a series of easy bounds, Jack and Beth caught up with him. Fabien went to dart past, back the way he'd come, but Beth put out her arm to block his path. He ducked away from her, yelping as his legs disappeared from under him and he tumbled onto the tiles. The packet dropped from his hand and slithered down the slope, coming to rest in the gutter amongst the dead leaves and moss.

For a second none of them spoke. Fabien's mouth twisted as if he was about to burst into tears, but instead he gave a low moan.

Beth slid down and squatted beside him. "You okay, Fabien?"

"My ankle." Fabien's teeth were clattering together.

"Let me look."

"No!" he sobbed. "Leave me alone."

"I won't hurt you." She leant forward. "I know first aid. Which ankle is it?"

"The left." The boy clutched his foot and gave another moan. "You scared me."

"You got a death wish?" demanded Jack. "Of all the dumb things . . . What are you doing up here?"

"Nothing. Nothing at all." Fabien's voice was shrill. Up close, Jack saw that dirt streaked the boy's face. Fabien shuffled backwards to prop himself against a chimney.

While Beth pulled Fabien's sock down and gently prodded his ankle, Jack retrieved the packet. He felt Fabien's eyes trained on him as he flipped it over. It was much lighter than the envelope they'd found the other day, but sealed the same way, with a double layer of parcel tape.

"I think you've twisted it," Beth said to Fabien. "You'll live."

Jack crouched in front of him, alarmed to see him trembling like a blade of grass. "What are you doing with this packet?"

A dribble of snot trailed from the younger boy's nose, and he gave a juddery sniff. "Please give it to me."

"What's in it?" Jack said. Fabien didn't answer, so Jack used his phone torch to examine the envelope, then ripped it open and stuck his hand inside. He brought out a velvet-covered box, finding a small watch with gold link strap inside. It was sparkly and clean, as if it had never been worn.

Beth whistled between her teeth. "Must be worth a fortune."

"Where did you get it?" Jack turned to Fabien, still holding the watch in his hand, an iciness creeping down his spine. "Come on, mate. You know you can trust us."

A spark of fear crossed the boy's face, his green eyes as round as buttons. Then he muttered something that Jack struggled to hear.

Jack crouched next to him. "What's that?"

"He'll kill me if I tell."

Jack stared at him. "Who?"

"It's obvious, Jack," said Beth. "He means Kai, don't you? You're stealing from The Willows and Kai's picking the stuff up."

Fabien took off his beanie hat and rubbed a shaky hand through his mop of sand-coloured hair, making it stand on end. "I'm not stealing. Not really. I don't even know what's inside the packets." His voice wobbled. "I take them from behind a pipe near the attic stairs and leave them between the chimneys. That's all."

"Who leaves them behind the pipe for you to pick up?"

"I've never seen them," sniffed Fabien. "Kai's never said."

"I don't get it," said Jack, frowning. "Why are you doing this?"

Fabien's gaze darted over the rooftops before settling back on Jack. Purple shadows stained the skin under his eyes and his freckles stood out like muddy specks on his pale grey cheeks. "When I was visiting Grandad a few weeks ago, I went to get a drink from the vending machine and took a shortcut down the back stairs. Kai was there, picking something up from behind a heating pipe. He was acting kind of weird – I don't know, suspicious . . ."

"And?" Beth said.

Fabien gave a half-sob. "He caught me watching, grabbed me around here –" Fabien gestured at his neck – "and said if I told anyone what I'd seen, he'd break my legs. Then he said I had to do exactly what he told me."

Something clicked in Jack's mind from their angry encounters with Kai on the rooftops over the summer. Had Kai been stealing from The Willows then? It would explain why he was so angry about finding them up there. He'd share his theory with Beth later, but right now they had the more urgent problem of Fabien to deal with. "Kai's got you doing his dirty work for him, so he doesn't risk getting caught?"

Fabien nodded and took another gulpy breath.

"He doesn't have a good reason for being in the home, but you do – to visit your grandad," said Beth, chewing her lip.

Fabien nodded again, rubbing his ankle. "He told me I only had to do it once. But now he says I have to do it whenever he wants. And if I don't . . ." He left the words hanging.

"How long's this been going on?"

"Two, three, four weeks maybe . . . I've lost count. One time the stuff got wet cos I forgot to put it in the bin liner. I got in a heap of trouble for it." He pulled up his shirt and showed them a vivid green bruise across his back. "It's what happens if I mess up." He pulled his shirt down again and tucked it into the waistband of his trousers. "Now I'm mixed up in it all, Kai knows I won't blab to the police."

"You've got to tell someone," said Jack gently. "Your mum or dad, your grandad . . ."

"I should have done that when it all started, but I didn't, and now it's too late." Fabien snuffled. "Anyway, what can Mum and Dad do about it? Go to the police? Kai will make sure I get the blame. And I don't want to worry them or Grandad."

A gust of wind scraped Jack's hair across his brow and he shivered. He quickly glanced up and saw that an ominous mass of slate-grey clouds had built up in the darkening sky, hanging like a huge alien ship over the city. "Mate, it can't go on."

"What can I do?" said Fabien. "I'll end up in prison. Who'll look after Grandad? And Bertie? He needs me. He only likes me to take him for his walks."

"Hey, you won't go to prison," said Jack, although he wasn't at all sure. What *did* happen to thirteen-year-olds who broke the law?

"And say Kai hurts Grandad?" said Fabien unsteadily. "I can't let that happen."

"We won't let that happen," said Beth, her black eyes flashing. "Kai won't get away with it."

Fabien fixed his pleading gaze on Jack. "If that packet isn't there when Kai turns up, I'm as good as dead."

Chapter Eight

Jack shifted his gaze between the packet and Fabien's pale face, then slowly got to his feet. Go to the police, that was what they should do. Let them deal with it. But what kind of trouble would that land Fabien in?

"I'll sort it." Jack made his way up to the chimney, stuffed the packet into the black bin liner he found up there, and wedged it between the pots. That would buy them some time to think about how to help Fabien. He returned to the others. Fabien was still looking green and shaky, but was on his feet and putting on his hat.

"I'll help you get down to the street," said Beth.

"It's okay. I'll go back through the attic. Grandad will be wondering where I am." The boy hobbled up the incline, back the way he'd come, and they heard him stagger down the other side.

Jack banged his fist against the chimney wall, sending loose cement dust showering onto the tiles. "I wish he'd told me what was going on. I could have helped. I wondered why he wanted me to teach him shadow jumping."

"He's scared," said Beth. "Don't be too hard on him. Kai's got him where he wants him. It's Kai you should be angry with, not Fabien."

"Who's Kai working for?" Jack let out a worried breath. "I mean, he might be a thug, but he's not got a lot of brains, has he?"

Beth pressed her lips together in thought. "You're right. He can't be doing this alone."

Jack's encounter with Kai from a few months ago was inked on his memory like a tattoo. He touched his ribs as if the bruising was still there, but of course the *physical* injuries were gone. Not so for Fabien, Jack thought, remembering the livid mark blooming on the boy's back. Kai wasn't the brains behind the thefts, no way. They needed to find out who he was working for. Find the mastermind, solve the crime, tell the police. "We can't stand by and do nothing. Let's wait for Kai to pick up the packet and follow him."

They concealed themselves behind a chimney pot on a neighbouring roof that gave them an unobstructed view of the drop-off place. It wasn't long before they saw the lumbering form of Kai approaching the chimneys. He carried a powerful torch, its beam throwing out light in a wide arc. With a quick glance around, he pulled the black bin liner from between the pots, took the packet out, stuffed the bag back, then headed down the slope.

The sun had set, the clouds obscured the moon from view, and light raindrops began to splatter Jack's face. They followed Kai, making sure they kept a safe distance and trod carefully – the tiles were treacherous when wet. Jack wished he could turn his phone torch on again, but to do that would give them away. No, they had no choice but to trust his skill on the rooftops.

Five minutes later, Kai veered left. Jack and Beth followed and were in time to see him vault over a low wall. Jack immediately recognised Kai's DIY rooftop terrace. It was where they'd run into Kai for the first time, last summer.

They hid behind the wall to watch. Light from the windows of the building spilt onto the concrete, illuminating the overturned crate seats Jack remembered from before. The old deckchairs, where he and Beth had been sitting when they'd first encountered a red-faced and fuming Kai, were still there too. A large plastic white tub sat next to one of the deckchairs, full to the brim with empty lager cans floating in scummy water. Others littered the ground, along with cigarette butts and empty crisp packets. Despite the coolness, a window in the building was open. Kai clambered through and disappeared inside.

Jack and Beth leapt over the wall and ventured nearer the window, ducking out of sight under the sill. Jack heard male voices coming from inside – one was Kai's, the other Jack couldn't quite place, although he was sure he'd heard it somewhere. The voices got louder then softer, as the breeze wafted garbled words in their direction, then snatched them away.

"Look at the state of this place," said the shouty, harsh voice. "You call this clean?"

"I haven't had time—" whined Kai.

"You're a good-for-nothing slob, that's what you are."

Kai muttered something indecipherable.

"Sponging off me all the time. Who gave you a roof over your head? Who fed and clothed you, eh? Who gave you work? Me, that's who."

Another mutter from Kai.

"Don't give me all that! You've cocked up. You're going to get us both caught. Want to end up in jail like my useless brother?"

"Dad's not useless," Kai bellowed.

The man gave a hollow laugh. "Like father like son, that's what I say. You had one job to do. One job. And what happens? You get caught by the first person who comes along." Jack's ears pricked up. Was he talking about Fabien?

"That window's too small for me. I thought . . . Sorry, Uncle."

"*Sorry, Uncle*," the angry voice mimicked. "You've jeopardised the whole plan with your stupidity. This is my future we're talking about. You'd better make sure that the boy doesn't blab."

"He won't. I'll deal with him."

The voices faded. Jack and Beth took the chance to peer over the windowsill into a large kitchen-diner. The room was empty. Jack tried to spot the brown envelope, but it was hard to see anything amongst the filthy dishes stacked on the draining board and worktops, and the takeaway cartons and pizza boxes piled on the table. Jack almost felt sorry for Kai, having to live in that tip with his nasty uncle. Almost. Suddenly Beth stood up.

"What're you doing?" Jack hissed in panic.

"Going inside," she whispered. "Kai's working for this uncle of his. We need to find out who he is. And there could be proof in there of what they're up to."

She was acting all impulsive again. Jack grabbed her arm and pulled her back down beside him. "It's too dangerous. They're still in there. Anyway, we have to act clever. There could be others involved. This could be massive."

Beth let out a frustrated huff, which ruffled her fringe. "We can't let them get away with it."

"We won't," said Jack, at the same time wondering exactly how they were going to stop Kai and his uncle.

A noise came from inside. They both peeped over the sill again. Kai was alone, shovelling the rubbish from the table into a bin bag. Jack gulped. Kai was even wider than he remembered. His neck muscles bulged over the edges of the T-shirt he was wearing, and the armholes were so tight it looked as if the material was cutting off the blood supply.

Jack gestured to Beth. There was nothing more to gain from hanging around, apart from getting caught. They crept away, across the terrace, over the low wall and onto the neighbouring rooftops. Only when Jack was sure they couldn't be seen from Kai's flat did he dare switch on his torch.

"Who is Kai's uncle?" said Beth as they clambered across the tiles. "And what did Kai mean when he said he'd 'deal with him'? I guess he was talking about Fabien."

"It doesn't sound good," said Jack with a shiver.

They reached a warehouse where they could make a short hop onto a lower roof and then to the alleyway below. It was an easy manoeuvre that Jack could have done with his eyes shut. Just as well, because it was now really dark. He shone the torch onto the roof so that Beth could see her way. Better safe than sorry.

"What about telling Malcolm and Nina what we've found out?" said Beth.

"Bad idea," he said, after watching her drop onto the roof below, then joining her. He checked that the large wheelie bins were still in place for their final move. "They might be involved too."

"You think?" Beth sounded doubtful. "I'm not sure Malcolm's got it in him to steal. And Nina *wants* the police to investigate. If we don't do anything, we're leaving Fabien in danger."

"But if we speak to them, Fabien could end up in prison along with Kai and his uncle." Jack crouched and dropped onto the lid of one of the bins, then to the ground. Beth followed.

"We have to do something," she repeated.

"I'll warn Fabien about Kai." Jack didn't want to freak Fabien out. Better to speak to him face to face, so he tapped a quick message, hoping it sounded urgent, but not enough to cause Fabien panic: *Need to talk about K. See you tomorrow in library.*

Jack and Beth made their way out of the alley and on to the main street. It had started raining heavily, and people rushed to and fro, trying to avoid getting drenched. A lorry went by, splashing rainwater that soaked Jack's trainers and socks before he had a chance to leap back. By the time they reached the traffic lights where they were to go their separate ways, he was dripping. It didn't do anything to improve his mood. Beth said goodbye, promising him she'd think up a plan to help Fabien. Jack hoped she would. She was always full of ideas. Fabien had trusted them with his terrible secret and Jack didn't want to let him down. He *couldn't* let him down. As he carried on home, the boy's scared, pasty face kept popping into his mind, while his words, "He'll kill me," reverberated in his ears.

Chapter Nine

Fabien's troubles played on Jack's mind all night, and he spent hours staring up at the night-time shadows stretching across the ceiling. Finally he dropped into an uneasy sleep, full of dreams of shady figures waving fistfuls of cash. The next thing, his alarm was squawking, demanding that he prise himself out of bed.

Jack's head ached. There was a thumping behind his left eye that even some painkillers Auntie Lil gave him couldn't fix, he had no clean shirts, and Mum called as he was about to leave the flat to remind him to use his sun cream. It meant he was late to school and didn't catch up with Beth until the end of the day, when he saw her spiky black hair bobbing up and down in the corridor amongst the throng of girls from her tutor group.

Beth wore her uniform in a slightly different way to Sadie and her other mates. The cuffs of her shirt were folded over the ends of the sleeves of her sweater. Her tights had a hole in them, her shoes were worn and dirty, but she didn't seem to care. Jack liked her scruffy retro look.

By the time Jack reached her, the other girls had disappeared, and Beth and Sadie were huddled together in front of a row of lockers, peering at something small and shiny in Beth's palm.

"Hey." Jack nudged Beth. She curled her fingers around whatever she was holding. His scalp tingled unpleasantly beneath his baseball cap.

"Hi, Jack," said Sadie, pushing her bouncy brown hair behind one ear and grinning.

"Hi." He matched her grin with a scowl. "What's that?" He focused on Beth's scrunched-up fist, trying to sound offhand.

"Tell you later." She crammed her hand into the pocket of her blazer, gave Sadie a quick hug and steered Jack away. "We've got more important things to talk about."

They ducked into a nearby classroom. Jack immediately pulled the window blinds down, blocking out the weak autumn sunshine. Beth sat on one of the desks, swinging her legs back and forth.

She scrutinised him. "You look terrible."

"Have you seen Fabien today?" said Jack, ignoring her comment. "He didn't turn up in the library."

She shook her head. "I looked for him everywhere. I'm worried."

"Me too." Jack exhaled. "I've messaged him again with a warning about Kai."

"But he wouldn't have had his phone switched on at school," said Beth, scrunching her black eyebrows together.

"Let's hope he turns it on before he gets to The Willows." Fear bubbled in Jack's throat and he gave a nervous swallow. "Did you think of a plan?"

"I think so," said Beth slowly. "But it means you doing a bit of spying."

"What kind of spying? Where?"

"We need to find out more before we go to Malcolm, right?" said Beth.

Jack nodded, not sure he liked where the conversation was going.

"And we need to act fast before Kai decides to 'deal with' Fabien," she said, making air quotes with her fingers. "If you're up for it." She paused as she studied his face. "Are you all right?"

"I'm fine," Jack lied. His headache had resurfaced with a vengeance, and his brain pounded against the plates of his skull. Swirly shapes zigzagged across his

63

vision. He pulled out his water bottle and took a quick swig.

"Okay. Let's go to The Willows." Beth pushed herself off the desk and led the way out of the classroom.

A few minutes later they'd left the school grounds and were walking along the street. Patches of cool sunlight bounced off the pavement, and as usual Jack hugged the shadows created by a row of shops, wary of the scorching sun.

"Kai's uncle is the key to everything," Beth explained as they crossed the street. "Maybe someone at the home knows Kai or his uncle. You snoop around, ask questions while I'm at the piano."

"But what am I looking for? And where? I can hardly search the whole place while you're playing Beethoven. I usually don't leave the lounge." Although Beethoven had written some really long symphonies, he thought to himself. "Malcolm and Nina will spot me and get suspicious."

"I'll invite them to listen to me playing. They won't be able to say no. That'll leave you free to snoop," said Beth. "Agreed?"

Jack shrugged a yes. It wasn't a brilliant plan. There were a hundred things that could go wrong, the main one being that someone would catch him. It would be a bit like when he and Beth had climbed onto the roofs of

Bioscience Discoveries in the dead of night to search for clues to Dad's whereabouts. It had all ended with a trip to the hospital for Jack when fleeing security. *But* Fabien needed their help, and, he had to admit, working together with Beth again would be cool.

By the time they'd finished talking through the flimsy plan in more detail, they were entering the hall of The Willows. Nina and Malcolm were at the front desk again. Nina wore an angry frown, and Malcolm was as sweaty and red as ever.

Nina clocked them straight away. "Just the people we need to speak to."

"Nina, love, I'm not sure now's the right time." Malcolm's words seemed to inflame Nina more.

"I disagree, Mal. Now *is* the time. They need to know."

"We need to know what?" demanded Beth.

"That you won't get away with it." Nina leant forwards over the reception desk towards Beth, propping her elbows on the top, her mouth a crimson slash across her powdered face. "We're on to you."

Chapter Ten

"You think *we've* been stealing?" Beth's mouth fell open. Two circles of bright pink had appeared on her cheeks.

"Of course Nina's not suggesting that," Malcolm hurried to say. "I'm sure we can sort it out—"

"Things are going missing," hissed Nina. "Valuable things . . . and money. It can't go on, it really can't."

"We know—" Jack began.

"Three people have started here recently," continued Nina. "Iris . . . and I can't imagine it's her. I don't like to point fingers, really, but . . ." She left her words hanging.

"Let's chat in my office." Malcolm cast a nervous glance at Nina, whose expression was as stony as the mantelpiece above the fireplace in the lounge. "I'll deal with this, love. You look after things here."

Nina muttered something under her breath, but thankfully, didn't object to his suggestion. Malcolm ushered them away.

"As if we'd steal," said Beth, as they hurried down the wide, gleaming corridor after the manager. "I can't believe you think that."

"It's not me," he reminded her. "Nina's just wound herself up, that's all. She'll calm down, you'll see."

Malcolm shepherded them past the portraits of regal-looking men and women from long ago, the alcoves housing semi-naked statues and pot plants, and the shiny antique tables. He pointed out things of interest along the way, as if it was their first time at The Willows and he was giving them a guided tour. Jack realised Malcolm was trying to ease the tension hanging in the air like a storm cloud. Any more on edge and Beth would have had steam coming out of her ears. Jack didn't feel much better. His head pounded, the pain drilling behind his eyes with every step he took.

They passed the lounge, restaurant and various doors labelled staffroom, toilets and storerooms one, two and three, heading towards the rear of the building, an area Jack hadn't visited much. On the way Malcolm greeted everyone they passed – residents, Ray the cleaner, restaurant staff and Jolly, the grumpy security guard. Through a fire door, Jack glimpsed a concrete courtyard and a row of enormous wheelie bins. Malcolm veered left into a narrower corridor, halted opposite the kitchen, "The most important place in the building," he told them, and was soon unlocking a frosted glass door with a key on a furry lion fob.

Malcolm steered them into his office. "Bit of a mess, I'm afraid." The light was on, the only window to the outside covered with sheets of yellowing newspaper. "For privacy," said Malcolm, to Jack's unspoken question. "I'm waiting for blinds to be fitted."

There was a large metal grey desk in the middle of the office with mounds of paperwork, scrunched-up tissues and mouldy apple cores scattered across its top. Cardboard files, piles of unopened letters and dirty coffee cups covered every other surface in the room. A spiral-bound manual entitled *Top Tips for Healthy Living in Later Life* was balanced on top of the brimming wastepaper basket by the desk.

The air smelt of stale cigarette smoke and Jack was starting to feel sick. He coughed, which sent another twinge shooting across his temples. Malcolm darted about as he attempted to clear the clutter, sweeping the tissues and apple cores into the bin, stacking papers into an untidy heap. "I suffer from allergies," he said, as if that explained why his office was such a dump. "All year round. Such a bore. And I don't seem to have time nowadays to keep on top of things." He waved them towards some chairs. Beth, who'd been scowling since Nina had confronted them in reception, took the hard-backed one, leaving Jack a worn-out armchair piled with books. He moved them onto the floor and sank down gingerly, his bum almost at the floor as the saggy seat all but gave way under him.

A shrill phone tune came from under the remaining stuff on the desk. Malcolm searched frantically through the papers. "Now, where on earth did I put it?" He picked up a stack of letters and shunted them onto the floor. The shrill got louder as Malcolm scurried about, picking this and that off his desk and then putting it back, until Jack found the phone under a vibrating letter heap.

"Great, thanks." Malcolm gave him a wide smile. He tapped the screen and held it to his ear. "I need to handle this." Sitting in the chair behind the desk, he swivelled his back to them, as if that would prevent them listening in.

"I understand, yes . . . but if you give me a little more time . . . I'm sure I'll be able to get it to you. Cash flow has been a bit of a problem this month, but I'm expecting a solution to that any day now. You'll get paid, I promise." There were more rushed words saying the same, and then he hung up. "Sorry about that. There's always something when you're trying to run a business . . . Now, where were we?"

"You were accusing us of stealing," said Beth stiffly.

"Now, now, it's all hot air with Nina." Malcolm got up, came round to their side of the desk and propped himself on the corner. "Some people have reported money going missing. It's also true that it began about the same time you started here. But that doesn't mean we think it was you."

"Nina does," Beth growled. "But we'd never do something like that. Ever."

"Exactly what I told Nina," said Malcolm. He plucked a tissue from a box and dabbed at his sweaty temples. "Of course, I believe you. But if you've heard or seen anything unusual, please tell me – it won't get you into trouble. It could help clear this whole matter up."

Beth picked at her thumbnail, as if debating what to do. Jack caught her eye and gave her a slight nod. She took a deep breath. "There *is* something—"

The office door crashed open and Nina flew into the room, her face as grey as the paint on the ceiling. She flapped her arms at Malcolm, shrieking, "Mal, Mal!"

"Whatever's wrong?" Malcolm rose from the desk and hustled her from the room. Their voices drifted in from the corridor outside, at first muffled, then louder . . .

"His poor family," Nina was saying, her voice cracking.

"What was the boy doing?"

"The police think he was fooling around. He wasn't alone, so eyewitnesses on the ground say. Though no one else's come forward."

A cold weight of dread dropped into Jack's legs. He struggled to get his leaden feet moving, but Beth was already out the door. When, at last, he'd prised himself from the chair and made it into the corridor, he came across Malcolm hugging a blubbing Nina, while Beth looked on, ashen-faced. Malcolm turned to them, his arm still around Nina. "You two will find out sooner or later anyway. It'll be on the news. A young lad's been found in one of the back alleys. He was seen on the roofs moments before he fell."

"Who is it?" Jack swallowed hard, his mouth suddenly as dry as sand. "Is he dead?"

"Keep your voice down," Nina hissed, as if Jack had yelled out. "We don't want the residents to hear. Not until we've had a chance to break the news gently to them."

"Take it easy, Nina," said Malcolm, and then to Jack, "It's Mr Garibaldi's grandson."

"Fabien?" Beth's horrified gaze landed on Jack.

Malcolm nodded. "You know him? I'm so sorry. A passer-by called the ambulance."

"Dead?" The word croaked out of Jack. He was super-aware of his pattering heart, his breaths coming shallow and rapid. He couldn't feel his fingertips and his head was about to explode, throbbing in time with his heartbeat.

Someone was speaking to him. Spots darkened his vision. The corridor started to spin.

He put his hands against the wall for support.

But it was too late. His legs buckled under him and he gave in to the blackness.

Chapter Eleven

Jack awoke flat out on the carpet, Nina kneeling beside him, fanning him with a pad of paper. The waft of air revived him a bit but didn't remove the thumping ache behind his right eye.

"Here, have a drink," said Malcolm. "You had a funny turn."

Jack struggled up, his head spinning, and shuffled back to prop himself against the wall. He took the plastic cup from Malcolm. The water was lukewarm and tasted vaguely of antiseptic, but he finished it in a couple of gulps. "Th-thanks. Please tell me . . . Fabien . . . ?"

"He's alive. Just," said Nina, moving the pad to fan herself. "Such a shock. Poor boy. He's in a coma. It could be brain damage. He might not recover—"

"He's unconscious, not in a coma," Malcolm cut in. "Don't scare the youngsters. He landed on a load of rubbish bags, which broke his fall." He glanced at Jack again. "How are you feeling?"

"Better." Jack swallowed, the still-dry sides of his throat rasping against each other. Nina was staring at him with a none-too-sympathetic look. He wobbled to his feet. His headache had cleared a bit and he no longer felt as if he was going to throw up, but he needed fresh air and to try to organise his muddled thoughts.

"Anyone at home able to pick you up?" said Malcolm, getting to his feet.

The last thing he wanted was Auntie Lil fussing around and then phoning Mum. "I'm fine, really," said Jack. "I can get the bus."

"Well, if you're sure." Malcolm's doubtful gaze switched to Beth.

"I'll go with him," said Beth, taking a grip of Jack's elbow. Her warm fingers squeezed his arm and her firm grip felt good, even though he didn't really need it.

"Yes, best you both leave," said Nina, also getting up.

Malcolm placed a hand on Beth's shoulder. "You're still welcome here. The residents love you. We'll sort out that other business, don't you worry."

Nina went back to the lobby with them and held open the main door. She scowled, a line ploughing the space between her drawn-on eyebrows. "Whatever Malcolm says, I'll be watching you. When the police come, they'll want to speak to you."

Nina's glare burnt into his back as he followed Beth out of the building. The fresh air revived him, but as soon as the doors thudded behind them and they were alone in the car park, Beth reeled round to him, her face crumpling, and black mascara tears trickling down her cheeks. A dribble of snot leaked from her nose and she gave a sniff. "We should have done something to protect Fabien."

"Maybe it was an accident." Even to his ears, the words sounded pathetic.

"Get real, Jack. Fabien wasn't alone on that roof. Witnesses saw someone else."

She was right, and she didn't need to say who. The only person who could have been on the roof with Fabien was Kai.

"Everything's going wrong. Fabien's unconscious; Nina's got it in for us. We can't tell Malcolm what we know about the thefts because it'll look as if we're blaming Fabien when he can't defend himself, just to save ourselves." She took a deep breath, then plonked herself on a low wall bordering The Willows car park. Jack joined her. She glanced over at him through puffy eyelids. "Fabien could have died, Jack. He might still die. And it'll be our fault." Her tearful words were darts, peppering his fragile skin, each one providing a fresh stab of guilt.

As they plodded home through the dark streets, Jack grew more and more miserable. Beth was right – Fabien could have died and might still. But *she* wasn't the one to blame. It was all *his* fault that Fabien was in hospital. Beth had wanted to tell Malcolm earlier. It was Jack who had said it was a bad idea. And he should have done more to help Fabien – he should have stopped him risking his life on the roofs when he was so badly prepared. He should have warned Kai off somehow.

Now it wasn't only Jack's head that hurt. His body ached as if he'd done a particularly hard stint of shadow jumping. Every muscle, joint and bone thudded and throbbed. But unlike the ache he had after jumping, he knew that this pain wouldn't go away after a decent night's sleep.

Chapter Twelve

He wasn't looking his best, Jack noted, as he applied his super-strong sun cream in the bathroom the following morning. The truth was, he'd hardly slept a wink. Every time he was about to drift off, a memory from the day before shocked him awake, his eyes pinging open and a fresh wave of misery rolling in. Spending the evening trying to find out how Fabien was hadn't helped. Jack had phoned the hospital on his way home from The Willows. It had taken ages to get through to the right department, and when Jack had finally managed to speak to someone, they'd told him they couldn't divulge information about a patient's condition to someone who wasn't a relative. He had called Mr G, but the phone just rang and rang. Maybe he'd gone with Fabien's parents to the hospital? If either Jack or Beth had known Fabien's parents' number, Jack would have left a message for them too. He had even rung Fabien's mobile, but the call had gone straight to voicemail.

Jack examined his face in the bathroom mirror. Purple shadows underscored each eye and his skin had turned zombie grey. Even Auntie Lil, who didn't usually notice stuff like that, said he looked "like the walking dead". She insisted he ate a big fry-up for breakfast. Normally he'd have wolfed it down, but that day his tummy was as unsettled as his thoughts.

At school the hours dragged by, but finally the end-of-day bell went and Jack rushed to the gates to meet Beth. He was desperate to see Mr G to make sure he was okay and to ask about Fabien – his grandad would surely know how he was. *And* they had to carry out Beth's plan and investigate the home. That would help Fabien, for when he woke up. Because he had to wake up, right?

Neither Nina nor Malcolm was in the reception area when he and Beth got there. One less problem to deal with at that moment. Jack didn't know how his and Beth's presence would go down with Nina. It was clear she didn't trust either of them.

Jack breathed a sigh of relief to see Mr Garibaldi in his usual spot on the long sofa in front of the fire in the lounge. Mr Garibaldi flashed a fleeting smile at Jack and Beth as they plonked themselves in the armchairs.

"I suppose you've heard Fabien's in hospital?" said the old man, his voice faltering slightly.

"Yeah, I'm really sorry. I'm . . ." Jack stopped, wishing he could sink further into the squidgy chair cushions. After all, he could hardly add, "And I'm the one who as good as put him there," could he?

"The hospital won't tell us how he is," said Beth. "Do you know?"

"They're hopeful he'll pull through, although he's still unconscious. Stable and comfortable, they say."

Stable, what does that mean? Jack felt another wave of worry. "That's good, right?"

"He's young and fit. I'm sure he'll recover just fine. But what the devil was he doing up on the roofs?" continued Mr G. "It doesn't make sense." The old man creased his wiry grey eyebrows together and exhaled noisily. "Do you know?"

Jack fixed his gaze on the Write a Will with Bill business cards still strewn across the coffee table, unwilling to meet Mr G's eyes. Unwilling to lie.

"Some kind of dare?" suggested Beth faintly.

"Does that sound like Fabien to you?" Mr G said. "He hates heights. He got scared going on the London Eye last year."

Of course, he was right. Fabien wasn't the type to do dares on rooftops, or anywhere else for that matter. Jack and Beth knew exactly what Fabien had been doing. But telling Mr G about it? What good would that do? Worry him when he couldn't solve the problem, that was what. No, it was best to say nothing until they'd found out who was behind all this.

"Fabien will be okay," said Jack weakly. "He's in the best place." He stopped. He was sounding like Mum again.

Mr Garibaldi didn't seem to notice the sudden silence. Instead, he plumped up the cushion at his back and settled himself more comfortably on the sofa. "No, it doesn't sound like Fabien at all," he repeated, seemingly to himself, and took a slurp of tea. "You're right, though. He'll be back with us before we know it."

With Mr G lost in thought, Jack turned his attention to Beth. Unusually for her, she wasn't saying anything. She fiddled with something glinting on a chain around her neck.

"That new?" Jack asked, realising that he hadn't seen her wearing it before.

"Not really. It was in the box of Mum and Dad's stuff the police gave me after the crash. I only found it the other day." She took off the chain from around her neck and showed it to him. A shiny brass key dangled from it. "It must have got stuck under a flap at the bottom of the box."

"What's the key for?" Jack asked.

"Don't know. We've been trying to come up with ideas."

"We?"

She took the key back, not looking at him. "Sadie and I."

Sadie again . . . That stung. His imagination instantly had them hanging out at Beth's place, sharing popcorn, chatting, having fun, solving the puzzle of the mystery key together . . . without him. "You could have asked me for help. Why didn't you tell me about it?" he grumped. He was being petty, but couldn't stop himself. Heat was prickling from the top of his scalp down the back of his neck, as if the sun had scorched his skin, though he was sitting well away from the windows.

Beth glowered at him through her black fringe. "I don't have to tell you every single thing. I bet there's loads of personal stuff you haven't told *me*."

His ears tingled. He couldn't think of a single thing about himself that Beth didn't already know. But then again, he hadn't had much of a life before he met her.

"May I look?" said Mr Garibaldi.

Ignoring Jack, Beth handed the chain to Mr G. He pushed his glasses further up his nose and inspected the tiny key. "Hmm, from a cash box or jewellery box, or a drawer of some kind, I suspect."

Beth nibbled her bottom lip as she took the key back and looped the chain around her neck again. "I wasn't planning on telling Sadie. But she noticed my chain and asked me what the key was for." Beth gave her fringe an impatient sweep with her hand. "And I've got nothing that belonged to Mum and Dad that needs a key like this. I don't even remember Mum having a jewellery box. It must be the key to something that was sold."

Jack attempted to push more mean thoughts about Sadie from his mind and said, "Or a safe deposit box?"

Mr Garibaldi shook his head. "Keys for those boxes are very distinct."

"What about the house or the garden shed?" said Jack.

"Shed keys are huge," said Beth. "Anyway, the house was sold over two years ago – after Mum and Dad died."

"But inside . . . a kitchen cupboard or wardrobe maybe. Something that would have been left in the house. It's a long shot, I guess—"

Beth grabbed Jack's arm so hard he yelped. "Sorry!" She loosened her grip and grinned. "But you could be right. Thanks, Jack!'

Jack shrugged, pleased. "No worries." Beth was beaming, and the Sadie-induced friction between them melted away.

"Teamwork, that's what it's all about." Mr Garibaldi gave a chuckle. "You two are doing a grand job of taking my mind off things and cheering me up." He leant to the side, fumbled in his waistcoat pocket and took out a bulky, folded handkerchief. He laid it on the table next to his mug. "Since we're sharing treasures . . . here's mine." Mr Garibaldi gave a quick glance around the room – no one was paying them the slightest attention – then pushed the white handkerchief towards Jack and Beth, with a nod of encouragement. "Go on, take a look."

Jack leant forwards and picked up the handkerchief. At first, he thought there was nothing inside, then he started to unfold it and his fingers encountered something small and hard. A sparkly blue gemstone about the size of a large pea dropped into his palm. For a moment, Jack and Beth were both lost for words, then Beth said, "Is it a . . . sapphire?"

Mr G shook his head. "It's a blue diamond. See how its colours catch the light? Breath-taking, isn't it?"

Jack rotated the stone in his hand, Beth craning forwards to see it too. The light danced and glimmered off the cut surfaces and the myriad of different shades of blue swirled inside. It was mesmerising.

"Is it real?" he asked.

"Real? Of course it's real!" bellowed Mr Garibaldi. "My father's great-great-grandfather brought it back from India in the seventeen hundreds, and it's been passed down from generation to generation ever since.

One day it'll be Fabien's. I was going to tell him that the other day, but then . . ." He sighed. "Anyway, the story goes that my ancestor once saved the life of an Indian prince, and he gave him the diamond as a reward. Rumour has it, the stone brings good luck to anyone who owns it." He gave a sudden deep chortle. "I'm still waiting for mine." He brought out a pen, picked up one of the Write a Will with Bill cards and wrote something on the blank side. "Fabien found the story about it on the interweb."

Curious, Jack glanced at the card, but Mr Garibaldi's writing was an illegible scrawl.

"Search for 'blue diamond' and 'Indian prince'," said Mr G.

Jack shoved the card in his trouser pocket. "I'll look for the website later. Is the stone worth a lot?" he asked.

Mr G waved a dismissive hand. "I expect so. But I'm not going to sell it."

A twinge of alarm shot through Jack. If the diamond was valuable, it would be a gift for the thieves. And here was Mr G, waving it around as if it were made of plastic.

Beth's jet-black eyebrows had crawled under her fringe. "Be careful, Mr G. Stuff's gone missing from people's apartments. There's a thief about."

"Oh my word! How do you know that?" The old man blinked rapidly at them behind his thick glasses.

"Malcolm told us. He's trying to keep it quiet so people don't panic," said Jack quickly.

"Your stone's beautiful, but you need to put it somewhere safe." Beth shuffled forwards in her seat. Linking her fingers together, she cracked her knuckles. "Seriously, Mr G."

"Don't worry, my dear. I've got the perfect place for it." He grinned with delight as Beth jumped up. "Are you going to play for us?"

"She's gonna try." Jack smirked. Beth shot him a hard look.

"Don't listen to him, Beth. You're marvellous, simply marvellous."

Beth pulled up the sleeves of her sweater and puffed out. "I'm a bit out of practice."

"Off you go." Mr G smiled. "We're looking forward to the concert, aren't we, Jack?"

"Jack can't listen today. He's . . . er . . . got to do a job," said Beth. She twitched her head towards the door, opened her dark eyes wide and pulled a silly face.

"What job?" He stared at her, his mind blank.

"You know . . ."

Beth did more manic face-pulling and head-jerking, and Jack finally remembered. He was supposed to be snooping. As Beth went to sit at the piano, Jack carefully put the stone back in the handkerchief and handed it to Mr Garibaldi.

"Beth's right," said Mr G, replacing the white bundle in his pocket. "I should put it in the safe at the bank. But what's the point of owning a gem if you hide it away?"

Jewels weren't really Jack's thing, but even he had to admit that the diamond looked impressive. His skin still tingled where it had sat in his palm. At that moment, Conchita came up with her trolley and began clearing used cups and plates off the table.

"Do you know someone called Kai?" Jack asked her. "He might have a relative here."

Conchita paused, plates in hand. "No, 'fraid not. Is he related to one of the apartment owners, or a member of staff?"

"I don't know," admitted Jack.

Conchita pursed her lips in thought. "The name doesn't ring a bell, but I haven't worked here long. What about you, Mr Garibaldi?"

Mr G rubbed at the stubble on his chin. "I can't say I've heard that name. Best ask Malcolm or Nina. What's this about?"

"Just asking for a friend," said Jack hurriedly. He sank back in his seat, wondering how he would get away to do some snooping.

Conchita finished stacking the plates. "We need more biscuits, Jack. Can you get some from storeroom one?"

It was the excuse he needed. Conchita rattled away and Jack glanced around the lounge. A crash of notes erupted from the piano as Beth began torturing it. The usual group of women at the little table by the window stopped their card game and turned to listen, while Mr Garibaldi leant back against the sofa cushions and closed his eyes. He looked as if he was nodding off, except his fingertips were tapping together in time to the erratic piano beat. Conchita had stopped in the middle of the room with the trolley, a rapt expression on her face.

Jack edged towards the door and slipped out of the lounge. Now was his chance to snoop around, while everyone was distracted by Beth's playing. He needed to get the biscuits, but first a little detour . . .

Chapter Thirteen

Jack paused outside the lounge, wondering where to try first. The route to the kitchens, Malcolm's office, the staffroom and the storerooms lay along the corridor to his right. Jack went left, soon reaching the wide hall and the reception desk. He was in luck again – the managers were still nowhere about, the hall deserted. Even so, he hung back, checking around, extra cautious. The only sound was the faint clang of Beth's piano playing. Next to the staircase nearest him, a sign read "Apartments 1 to 12" with an arrow pointing up to the galleried landing.

The soft, thick, cherry-coloured carpet muffled any noise his trainers made on the steps. Once at the top, Jack had the choice of going left or right around the landing. To the left were apartments one to seven, to the right lay apartments eight to twelve, according to another sign nailed to the wall. He opted to go left.

More old paintings hung on the walls of the landing, and each little alcove was filled with either an antique table or a leafy plant, like on the ground floor. Within a few metres another passageway led off the landing towards the rear of the building. There was another sign telling him the apartment numbers, this time numbers one to five. He dithered at the entrance to the passageway. What if he got caught up here? The biscuit excuse was weak – he was on the wrong floor and nowhere near the storerooms. As if someone had heard his thoughts, a door opened further down. Jack dived around the corner to hide, his heart cantering. He peeped out in time to see Jolly pull the door shut, quickly glance in both directions and hurry away. Had the security guard seen him? Jack prayed he hadn't.

Once Jack was sure Jolly wasn't coming back, he hurried to the apartment Jolly had left. A brass number two, a bell and a name card in a holder were fixed on the wall: Mrs Joyliffe, it read. What had Jolly been doing in Mrs Joyliffe's apartment? Jack made a snap decision, rang the bell, stepped back and waited. It shrilled inside. No answer. He rang again, this time keeping his thumb hard on the button, creating an angry screech. Not one sound came from the apartment – no shuffling footsteps, no slamming doors, nothing. He crept away, thinking hard. Jolly had looked guilty. Why would the security guard let himself into the flat when there was no one there? Unless . . . Jack gulped . . . unless he was the thief!

A door further up the corridor opened, and he heard voices. In panic, he spun round the way he'd come, tripping over his shoelace in his rush and stumbling into the wall. He put out a hand to steady himself, but his shoulder thudded against the front door of another apartment. He inhaled sharply and squeezed his eyes shut, praying that nobody was in, but the door flew open as if the person had been standing right on the other side. Jack's luck had run out. A bouncy, energetic-looking woman with tidy white hair cut in a line a centimetre below her earlobes peered out at him. "Hello?"

Jack's mouth flapped opened and closed, his mind suddenly a blank. "Uh, hello," he managed at last. In desperation, his gaze shifted sideways to the little card next to the bell that read: "Mrs Harper". He cleared his throat. "Hi, Mrs Harper, I was looking for Jolly."

The woman stared at him, puzzled. "Have you tried the security office?"

"Uh, I've been there."

"What do you want him for?" Mrs Harper opened her door wider, revealing a hallway decorated with dazzling striped black, white and grey wallpaper, and a silver carpet. "Have you been robbed too?"

Before Jack could answer, her gaze slipped past him. "Ah, Malcolm," Mrs Harper said. "There you are. I'd like a word."

Jack twisted round, his heart dropping into his belly, and came face to face with the manager.

"I hope this chap isn't making a nuisance of himself," said Malcolm, clapping Jack a little too hard on the back. "Lost?"

"Looking for the library. Mr Garibaldi wants me to get him a book," said Jack in a rush, before remembering that wasn't what he'd told Mrs Harper.

"Back down the stairs, and to the left of the restaurant," Malcolm replied. "You can't miss it." He gave a look that said, *How on earth did you miss it?*

"Right, sorry."

"Never mind the boy," said Mrs Harper. "That's not why I called you. I put my watch in the drawer and now it's gone."

Jack's ears pricked up at this new piece of information.

"Are you sure you haven't mislaid it? It's so easy to do," said Malcolm, sounding worried.

"I've told you before – one of your cleaners has got light fingers. It's been stolen and—"

"I'm sure there's an innocent explanation," Malcolm cut in. "Shall we talk inside?"

He threw Jack a sharp look, and Jack felt the tips of his ears become a guilty red-hot. Was *he* now Malcolm's prime suspect? He moved slowly away, not wanting to hang around and be interrogated further about exactly what he was doing on the first floor. At the same time, he strained to hear Malcolm and Mrs Harper's conversation.

"It's worth a lot of money—"

"I'll check with Ray. Maybe he's seen it lying around."

"Alan gave it to me for our fortieth wedding anniversary . . ." The voices died away as the apartment door slammed.

Jack hurried back downstairs, mulling over what he'd witnessed. Malcolm had been acting weirdly. What was his real reason for wanting to keep the thefts quiet? A guilty conscience? Or was he worried about his business? Then there was the security guard, Jolly. Surely he didn't have permission to go in and out of the apartments whenever he wanted? And what about Mrs Harper's claim that the cleaner had stolen her watch? Was Ray the man he and Beth had heard in Kai's flat? Or had it been Jolly? Was one of them Kai's mysterious uncle? Who could they ask? Malcolm? Nina? Jack couldn't imagine either of them being helpful, especially if they were somehow involved in the thefts, or even if they just thought he and Beth were the thieves. Perhaps Jack could ask the chefs, or one of the restaurant staff? So many questions, so few answers. With his head still spinning, he went back downstairs.

In the nick of time, Jack remembered the biscuits. He hurried to storeroom one, next to the kitchen, punched in the special security code Nina had given him when he'd first started at The Willows and pushed the door. The light pinged on automatically as he entered, and he faced floor-to-ceiling shelves stacked with different kinds of food in packets, jars, tins and boxes. Handily, the shelves were labelled, and he soon found a packet of digestives, ticked it off on the list behind the door, and scooted back into the corridor.

The frosted glass door of Malcolm's office opposite the kitchen was firmly shut, but there was a blurred shape moving around in the room. Jack froze. Malcolm was with Mrs Harper. He'd left them together only a couple of minutes ago. The manager couldn't have got back that quickly. So who was in his office? Nina? Jolly? He kept away from the glass and crept as close as he dared towards the door. Muffled metallic scraping came from inside, followed by a thud. Seconds later there was a series of flashes. Jack counted fifteen in total. Then a crackle of paper, a pause and another thud. The blurred shape moved nearer. Jack needed to get going. His heart thumped as he darted into the kitchen, then strained to see through a chink in the door.

The office door opened . . .

"What are you up to?" Jack spun round, coming face to face with a man in chef whites.

"Biscuits." He held up the packet, the back of his neck tingling unpleasantly. "Conchita asked me to get them."

"You've found them, so hop it," said the surly man. "Unless you want *me* to find you something to do."

Jack didn't need to be told twice. As he stepped out of the kitchen, he glanced in both directions. The corridor was empty. Apart from one person. Somebody was heading away from Malcolm's office towards the reception.

A familiar figure.

But the last person Jack expected to see.

Chapter Fourteen

Jack's mind was still reeling as he returned to the lounge, gave the biscuits to Conchita and dropped into the chair next to Mr Garibaldi. Beth was giving a final clattering flourish on the piano.

"Seen a ghost?" said Mr Garibaldi, scrutinising Jack.

"Something like that," he murmured, attempting to pull his chaotic thoughts together. Beth wandered back over.

"Lovely playing, as usual." Mr G gave her a warm smile as she sat on his other side.

"Thanks. But I stumbled a bit."

"Nonsense. It was wonderful," Mr G assured her.

Beth grinned, looking pleased, and turned to Jack. "Fancy a bus ride tomorrow?"

Despite his worries, Jack was curious. "Where to?"

"You'll see. Meet me at the bus stop after school." Her phone beeped. She swiped the screen to read the message. "I've gotta go."

"Me too," said Jack, shooting Beth what he hoped was a *we need to talk* look. He was bursting to tell her what he'd seen from outside Malcolm's office. After saying goodbye to Mr Garibaldi, they left the lounge and hurried to the exit.

Jolly was standing guard in the reception area. He looked as if he'd been waiting just for them. "Right, you two. Over here, please."

Jack shrugged at Beth and they went over to the desk. "What's up?"

"Bag check," said the security guard. "Orders of the management." Beth and Jack exchanged alarmed glances. *Orders of Nina, more like*, thought Jack.

"You can't search my bag unless I give you permission," said Beth.

Jolly raised an eyebrow. "True, but that makes it look as if you've got something to hide . . . Have you?"

Beth gave him a sour look and they both dumped their backpacks on the desk.

"As if I haven't got enough to do without this," grumbled Jolly, as he unzipped Beth's bag and rifled inside.

"Are you searching the residents' apartments too?" asked Jack, his brain ticking over.

"Course not," said Jolly, turning to Jack's bag. "Only people who work here." So that wasn't why Jolly had been in that apartment . . .

At last Jolly seemed satisfied that Jack hadn't got anything in the pockets of his bag apart from broken pencils, scraps of paper and a handful of chocolate bar wrappers, and told them to get going.

They didn't need telling twice and sped out of the building and into the street, as the cathedral bells were chiming 5.30 p.m. It was later than Jack had realised. It must've been raining while they were inside because the pavement glistened under the glow of the street lamps. He jerked his blazer collar up, feeling the damp chill around his ears and the cutting breeze ruffling his hair.

"Well?" Beth glanced sideways at him, her eyebrows knotted together. "Did you find out who Kai's uncle is?"

"No," he said, irritated. Trust her to pick on the one thing he hadn't managed to do. "But I've got other stuff to tell you." As quickly as possible, he explained what had happened, including Jolly's suspicious behaviour and the conversation he'd overheard between Mrs Harper and Malcolm about the cleaner.

"So Jolly could be the thief? How does he get into the apartments? A security guard for the building wouldn't have keys to everyone's homes." Beth quickened her pace as she talked and Jack struggled to keep up with her.

"It could be Ray. A cleaner would have keys," said Jack. "Although it's a pretty idiotic thing to do when you'd be the first one to be suspected of theft."

"We're getting closer to the truth."

"Are we?" said Jack. It felt to him as if they were further away than ever.

"Sure. Kai's uncle, who is either the cleaner or Jolly, does the stealing and leaves it behind the pipe for Fabien to pick up. Fabien takes it out via the rooftops to be picked up by Kai."

"I don't know. If it was Ray, why wouldn't he just take the stolen stuff out with the rubbish? He could hide it in a bin liner."

"What about Jolly then? He's less suspicious than a cleaner. And he has access to the security cameras. He could easily delete any evidence."

Jack was still doubtful. "That doesn't explain how he gets into the apartments. How come he had a key? He *could* mess with the cameras, but why would he get Kai or anyone else involved in removing the stuff from the building? All he needs to do is walk out with it through the front door. He's hardly going to search himself, is he?"

Beth pursed her lips, then gave a big sigh. "You're right. Just when I was thinking we were getting somewhere."

Jack took a deep breath. "There's more."

Beth stopped dead, her face reflecting the pale orange of the street lights. "What?"

Jack stopped too, twisted to face her, then told her what he had witnessed from outside Malcolm's office. "I saw my neighbour, Mrs Roberts!"

"Are you sure?"

"Course I'm sure. And I think the flashes were from a camera."

"But . . . what on earth was Mrs Roberts doing at The Willows? Why was she in Malcolm's office? What was she taking photos of?"

"Keep your voice down." Jack glanced around, half expecting Mrs Roberts to peel herself like a chameleon from the brick wall next to them.

"We've got to tell Malcolm. This changes everything." Beth reached for her phone.

Jack grabbed her hand to stop her. "Best to keep it quiet for now."

"Why?"

"Just because Mrs Roberts was in his office doesn't mean she has anything to do with the thefts."

Beth gave a frustrated huff. "Why else would she be in there? And why would she be taking photos?"

Something stirred in Jack's memory. "Didn't Nina mention something about an 'Iris' volunteering? That's Mrs Roberts's name."

"But I've never bumped into her, have you? Anyway, you reckon that gives her a right to be in Malcolm's office? I don't think so."

Another thought slammed into Jack. *That* was what had been bothering him when he saw Mrs Roberts in her flat the other day. Usually when he talked to her, he'd have to shout to get her to hear him. So why, when she was so deaf, had she been whispering into her phone? He told Beth what he thought.

"She's pretending to be deaf?"

"I know it sounds ridiculous. You'd think I'd have noticed something before now." Jack gave his hair an annoyed scrub with a hand. "I might have got it all wrong." His life seemed to be full of instances when he'd jumped to the wrong conclusions. Like the time he was convinced he'd spotted Mrs Roberts in Colford, when he was staying with Auntie Lil. He'd thought she'd been following him, spying on him for the director of Bioscience Discoveries. He'd been told he'd got it all wrong. But had he? "If we tell Malcolm this and he doesn't believe us, it could make things worse for us and for Fabien. We've got to have some kind of proof. Besides, how do we know Malcolm's not in on it?"

"We're assuming the thief has a connection with The Willows, otherwise how else would they know what to steal? Somebody there must know who Kai's uncle is."

Jack nodded, trying to collect his scrambled thoughts together. At every mention of Kai, he got a sick jolt as he pictured Fabien lying injured in his hospital bed. He had to find out the truth. "I'll keep asking around."

"But quietly." Beth's phone beeped. As she glanced at it, Jack glimpsed a string of messages.

"Cathy's taking me and Sadie out for a pizza," she said, catching him looking and blanking the screen. She sounded defensive.

"Can't you say you'll be late?"

"I'm *already* late." Beth went to turn away.

"What's so great about Sadie all of a sudden?" Jack burst out.

"I can't believe it, you're jealous!" Her tone was spiky.

"Course not," Jack spluttered, at the same time feeling his cheeks redden.

"Sadie's a friend." Beth went to say more, but this time her phone rang. "Hi. Yes, I'm on my way. See ya."

With a grunted bye to Jack, Beth stalked off. Jack kicked out at an empty cola can lying on the pavement,

101

making it spin into the road. A trickle of brown liquid fizzed on the tarmac and dribbled into the drain. A woman with a toddler glared at him, pressing the kid closer to her side as they passed. Jack buried his hands deeper into his pockets and shuffled off, acting like a guilty criminal.

A niggling doubt burrowed deeper and deeper inside him, like a worm. Perhaps Beth was right – he was a tiny bit jealous of her and her new life without him. He found it hard to trust people, but he trusted Beth. Beth had never stared, never been revolted by his grease-coated skin, never treated him like dirt stuck to the bottom of her shoe. She accepted him as he was. And he accepted her. So why did he feel that there was a barrier between them now, as thick as the cathedral walls? Maybe the truth was that he needed Beth more than she needed him.

Chapter Fifteen

The way they'd left things the previous afternoon, Jack wasn't sure Beth would turn up at the bus stop after school. But when he arrived, she was already there. She'd changed out of her uniform into her usual black leggings, hoodie and jacket. He wished he'd done the same, but he didn't want to go home and get stuck talking to Auntie Lil, so he'd hung around in the school library until it was time to meet Beth.

"I've been waiting ages," said Beth. "Where've you been?"

While in the library, Jack had hidden from the beady eyes of the librarian and sneaked a call to Mr G for an update on Fabien. "He had a comfortable night," Mr G had told him. Mr G had sounded fine, upbeat even, but Jack wasn't sure whether the news about Fabien was good or bad. Beth didn't have any doubt.

"That's good news," she said firmly. "You've got to be positive."

Being positive wasn't easy, but Beth was right. Jack shrugged his shoulders back – he had to stay strong for Fabien *and* Mr G. "So, what's the big mystery? Why are we here?"

"We're going to my old house."

Jack's stomach swooped – Beth had asked him to go with her. *Him*. Not Sadie. She'd chosen *him*. That felt good.

Beth knew which bus to catch, and within forty minutes they were standing on a road by a row of Victorian semi-detached houses, on the outskirts of the city. The houses at the top of the street all had neat front gardens, window boxes filled with plants and flash cars parked outside. As they made their way further down the road, the houses got scruffier. A man was sitting on a plastic chair outside one, a bottle of something in his hand. Light spilling from the house revealed that he was wearing nothing but shorts, an old grey vest, and a pair of dirty wellies, despite the biting wind. He flicked a look at them, then burped loudly as they hurried past.

Beth stopped outside a house with a For Sale sign outside. Under the yellow of the street lamps it looked like all the others. They went up the garden path edged by a tangle of weeds and long grass, and Jack noticed the downstairs windows had the inside shutters pulled closed.

"Mum and Dad bought it really cheaply from an old couple. They planned to do it up," said Beth, as if needing to explain its current state. "They never got the chance. I wonder what happened to the people who bought it after Mum and Dad died. I can't believe it's still in a mess." She raised the knocker on the chipped black front door and let it drop. The sound echoed emptily inside the house.

"Doesn't look as if anyone's lived here for a while," she said sadly.

"Better for us," Jack said, trying to sound cheery, though the run-down house gave him the jitters. "Is there a way in round the back?"

Beth pointed to the left, and they followed the concrete path winding around the side of the house. They stopped at the back door and tried the handle. The lock was busted; the splinters of wood looked fresh and pale, as if recently done. Jack shuddered – if ghosts existed, this would have been the kind of place they'd hang out.

The door creaked open with a light push and they stepped into the kitchen. It was dark, cold and smelt of fish. Beth flicked the light switch but nothing happened, so Jack got his phone out and tapped the torch app on, flashing the beam around.

Beth wrinkled her nose. "It stinks in here."

Jack's skin chilled, goosebumps tingling down his arms. He sincerely hoped there wasn't a dead body waiting to be discovered. The kitchen was filthy, with empty takeaway containers, tins, crisp packets and drinks cans strewn all over the place. Jack peered into a carton on the worktop. Inside was the remains of a Chinese noodles dish. Recent, by the look of it.

"Do you think anyone's in here now?" whispered Beth.

They both stopped and listened. Apart from his heartbeat walloping in his ears, Jack couldn't hear a sound, not even a dripping tap. Still, he didn't want to hang around. Whoever had made that mess could return at any second. His heart still pounding, he stepped further into the room. Something sticky had been spilt on the floor and nobody had bothered to wipe it up.

"I used to do my homework in here," said Beth from behind, her voice wobbling. "Mum would sing to the radio while cooking the tea, and I'd sit at the table. Mum was a terrible singer. Now it's home to squatters."

Jack reached out and squeezed Beth's arm, not sure what to say to make her feel better.

She sniffed and rubbed her nose. "Let's check the cupboard in the sitting room first."

Jack lit the way into the narrow hall leading to the front of the house. The bare floorboards were gritty from a broken glass bottle at the bottom of the stairs. The air was chilly and damp. His teeth started to chatter and he clenched his jaws together to make them stop.

"Hello?" Beth called out, as if expecting someone to answer. An echo boomed back through the empty house.

She led the way into the sitting room. There was no furniture at all, although there was an old carpet on the floor. Beth paused in the doorway and surveyed the room. "We had a piano in here, over by the window. It was where I learnt to play." She crossed the room and threw open the wooden shutters. Weak light from the street lamp outside pooled across the floor. "I had lessons and everything. Dad was the musical one; Mum was more interested in science."

Jack felt a jolt of sadness. It must have been hard for Beth to revisit her old home, with memories of her family crammed into every corner of every room. *His* parents were alive, although Dad lived in Aberdeen. That was hard enough. How much harder must it be to know that you'd never ever see your mum and dad again? Jack flicked a look at Beth. "Are you all right?"

"Yeah, I'm fine." Her voice cracked, but she was already moving towards the built-in cupboard by the fireplace. She huffed with disappointment when the key didn't fit that lock, and sat back on her heels in front of the empty grate. "The only other place is in my mum and dad's old bedroom."

They returned to the hallway, ready to go upstairs. A thud came from somewhere above them, followed by the unmistakable tread of footsteps crossing the landing. Beth took a pace back, bumping Jack's hand. His phone clattered to the floor and the torch went out, plunging them into darkness. He crouched, groping this way and that over the grimy floor. He remembered the broken glass too late – something sharp stabbed his fingertip and he felt the wetness of blood. Then he touched the smooth case of his mobile and picked it up as feet pounded down the stairs. Beth gave a frightened yelp. Jack fumbled with the torch app again and someone barrelled past him, hollering something. Jack was caught off balance and stumbled, his skull thwacking against the wall. He didn't have time to recover before Beth was pulling him to his feet, into the kitchen, then out of the house and through the garden. Whoever had scared them had disappeared into the evening.

"Are you okay?" said Beth, as they reached the pavement.

"It's just a scratch," Jack puffed. His bumped head hurt, but his hand worried him more. The torchlight showed his palm smeared with blood, and a cut slicing the tip of his little finger. He winced as he sucked the blood off. For his delicate skin, an injury like that could quickly turn into something from a horror movie.

"Oh, that's not good . . ." Beth grabbed his hand and peered at the wound. "You need to wash it. Let's go."

He didn't argue. The cold, gloomy house was giving him the creeps. "We'll come back when no one's about."

"Thanks for helping me," said Beth, giving him a small smile. Jack's cheeks burnt hot.

A couple of cars went by, their lights dipping and rising as they went over speed bumps. It was strangely quiet for that time of day. Even the man sitting outside his house had disappeared. Maybe the cold had made people hurry straight to their warm homes after work. For a moment Jack wished *he* was already safe at home with nothing to worry him, instead of hurrying to the bus stop with a cut finger, a bruised skull, and a mind bursting with problems he wasn't sure he could fix.

Chapter Sixteen

"Is that you?" called Auntie Lil as Jack slammed the front door an hour later and sloped into the sitting room, dumping his bag by the TV. She appeared in the kitchen doorway, her dyed blonde hair piled high, hands encased in a pair of oven gloves. "No kiss for me then?"

Auntie Lil ditched the gloves to draw him close, the top of her head just reaching his chest. It was only when she released him that he could breathe again. Then she caught sight of his hand. The cut, which had stopped bleeding on the journey home, had opened up. Blood plopped from his little finger onto the rug. "How on earth did you do that?"

"I don't know." Auntie Lil would accept that answer – his skin was as fragile as tissue paper. "I'm going to clean it now."

Auntie Lil rooted in the sideboard drawer and handed him a box of plasters. "Your mum called me from the hotel. Everything's fine, but she wants to chat. She's left a message on your phone."

Jack went into the bathroom, washed his hands, wiped the cut with antiseptic and applied a plaster. Minutes later he was in his room. Auntie Lil had been tidying up. His pile of dirty pants and socks had gone from the floor and cold air blasted through the open window. Out of habit, he shut the window and closed the thick curtains, to protect his skin from the sun – not that sunlight was a problem on a dark November evening.

He dumped his school shirt in the laundry bin, putting on his jeans and favourite hoodie – the one with the words "Do or Die" on the front and "Live it" on the back. He dug his phone out, rang his voicemail and listened to Mum's message. *"Hi, love. How're things? Hope you're staying out of trouble. Call me when you get this. Love you!"* Guilt nudged Jack as he wrote a quick text saying he was busy with homework. A lie, but the truth was he couldn't face one of Mum's inquisitions. And the last thing he seemed to be doing was staying out of trouble.

Jack left his room and was about to wander into the kitchen when his phone vibrated. A video call from Dad. Jack didn't want to speak to Mum, but Dad was a different matter.

"How're you doing, mate?" Dad sounded and looked as if he was in the next room, not hundreds of miles away in his lodgings in Aberdeen.

"Wait a sec." Jack whisked the phone back into his bedroom, flicked the light on and slammed the door.

"Bad timing?" his dad asked. "I can call back later."

"No, I'm good." A call from Dad was the last thing he'd expected, having seen him only a few days ago. He suspected Mum had put Dad up to it, to check up on him, but that didn't matter. It wasn't long ago that Dad seemed to have disappeared off the face of the earth. So a phone call was always a good thing. They spent the next ten minutes talking about Dad's search for a flat to rent because he needed his "own space", and about the job he'd started earlier that year, which he loved. A lot of what he told Jack about his investigations into new cancer treatments went right over his head. Dad's old job had been researching into anti-ageing drugs and had led Jack to thinking, wrongly, that his dad had experimented on children, including Jack. That was a memory Jack wished he could forget.

"The lab only shuts down for a couple of days, and by the time I get down to you and back up here again, I'll have spent all the time travelling . . ."

"What?" Jack's mind snapped back to the present.

"I know it's disappointing, but I'm in the middle of some really important stuff and my boss wants me around . . ."

"You're not coming for Christmas?" said Jack dully. Not again. Dad had always been a workaholic. Even so, he had promised that he'd be around more, especially since Jack had got so worried about him earlier in the year.

"I'm disappointed too, mate. The good thing is that I'm owed time off, so I'll have over two weeks to take in January. If your mum will put up with me that long. If it's a problem, I can stay in a bed and breakfast." Dad ran a hand through his thick hair. Things were better than they had been between Mum and Dad since they separated, but not so good that they wouldn't be at each other's throats after sharing the same space for more than a few hours.

"I'll be at school in January."

"Well, we'll have time when you get home, and the weekends."

"Great," said Jack. He tried, but he couldn't sound happy.

"So, what news do you have?" said Dad, filling the silence.

"Nothing big." Jack's belly flipped over. His worries about Beth, Fabien and everything going on at The

Willows were crowding in on him, but confiding in Dad during a video call, with hundreds of miles separating them, was not going to happen. And Jack didn't want to contribute to Dad's stress. He'd been getting therapy and insisted he was getting better. There was no way Jack was going to say anything to put his recovery at risk. No way. Anyway, how could he tell Dad about the horrible events of the last few days? His stomach churned at the thought of it – the guilt for what had happened to Fabien would never go away.

Dad arched his eyebrows. "Really? You're not saying much. Studying hard?"

"Er, yeah," Jack lied again, guiltily thinking of the pile of unfinished homework in his bag.

"And Beth?" Dad was probing now, like Mum did.

"She's great."

After that, the conversation pretty much dried up, and they soon ended the call.

Auntie Lil was standing at the hob stirring a pan when Jack entered the kitchen. "How was your day?" she said. A rich, meaty smell drifted towards him and his tummy growled.

"Fine."

"Get the bread out of the oven for me, will you?" said Auntie Lil, throwing him the oven gloves. "I had a lovely morning shopping, and then I bumped into your neighbour outside," she said. "Such a nice woman. She invited me in for a coffee. Turns out her sister lives near me . . ."

"You had coffee with Mrs Roberts?" Jack stopped dead, oven gloves on his hands.

"Why are you shocked at that idea, Jack? Iris is great fun. She was asking what you're up to nowadays. I mentioned about you volunteering at The Willows. She was really interested in that."

I bet she was. He tipped the bread from its tin onto a wire rack, plonked himself down at the table and zoned out as Auntie Lil jabbered on about this and that. All he could think about was Mrs Roberts. Why had she been in Malcolm's office? What did she take photos of? Was she gathering information for the criminal masterminds? He got to his feet.

"Where are you going?" said Auntie Lil.

"Next door."

"What on earth for? It's nearly dinner time!"

"I'll only be a minute."

Before she could question him further, he darted out of the flat, pulling the front door closed behind him. He stood in the corridor across from Mrs Roberts's, his thoughts swinging back and forth like a saggy zip wire. What would Beth do right then? Jack's gaze fell upon a toolbox on the floor of the corridor by the fire extinguisher, obviously left by a maintenance worker. It gave him half an idea. He wiped a sweaty palm down his jeans and rapped hard on Mrs Roberts's door. Seconds later there was the rattle of a chain, the door cracked open and a wrinkled face stared at him through the gap.

"Oh, it's you," said Mrs Roberts. She spoke loudly, her crinkled lips parting into a grey-toothed smile. Another rattle, and she opened the door wide. He saw the mobile in her hand. "What can I do for you?"

"My aunt wanted to know if you had a –" Jack licked his lips – "hammer . . ."

"A what?"

"Hammer," he said more loudly this time.

"That's kind of her, doing DIY for your mum." Jack gave a one-shoulder shrug, but said nothing. Better that than dig himself into a deeper hole. He'd have to hope Mrs Roberts didn't decide to have a conversation with Auntie Lil later about exactly why she needed a hammer.

"Wait there, then." Mrs Roberts turned, dropped her phone into a drawer in the cluttered little table in the hall and shuffled towards her sitting room. "Now, where would I have put it? I might be a while . . ."

Here's hoping, Jack thought. He slipped inside the flat and grabbed Mrs Roberts's phone from the drawer. With a jolt he realised it was one of the super-sleek new Comet models, not the basic type he'd expected the old woman to have. There was no time to consider that fact though – he had to get to work. Luck was on his side for once – the screen hadn't locked. He tapped the gallery icon. Empty. He searched the files folder, downloads, and every other place he could think of which might hold the photos she'd taken at The Willows. But there was nothing. He swore under his breath – there'd be no way of finding them now. What also bothered him was that there was nothing personal on her phone at all. No texts or messages, no files, no emails. Nothing. He heard Mrs Roberts banging about in the sitting room. Any second she'd be back. In a last-ditch effort to find anything of use, he tapped on the contacts list. The last call she'd made was to a 0141 number. He fetched out his own phone and took a quick snap of the screen, then placed hers back in the drawer and hopped back into the corridor as Mrs Roberts reappeared.

"Is it the right type?" she bellowed, handing him something that looked as if it wouldn't bang a nail into jelly. "Tell your aunt she can keep it for emergencies. I've got another. There's nothing worse than not having a hammer." Jack did a double take. Had she winked at him?

"Thanks." He slipped the tiny hammer into his jeans pocket.

"How's the volunteering going? Your aunt told me about it."

Here was his chance to probe. "It's great. You help there too, don't you?"

Mrs Roberts's pinprick eyes widened. "Now and then, yes. I teach bridge and run tai chi classes, that sort of thing."

Tai chi? It was some kind of exercise, wasn't it? An image of Mrs Roberts wearing her pink, fluffy slippers in a tai chi pose popped into his mind. Too late, a laugh burst from his mouth. Mrs Roberts gazed at him in alarm. He was saved by her phone going off, and she waved him away in apology, shutting the door.

Chapter Seventeen

Thoughts were whirling round Jack's head. He needed some space to think things through, so after dinner he decided to get out of the flat. It was a cold evening with a squally wind that wafted piles of dead leaves across the path as he hurried through the park. Jack went over what he'd learnt at Mrs Roberts's. He'd been right – Mrs Roberts *did* volunteer at The Willows. At last, they were getting somewhere. He hadn't found the photos, but he had a phone number. It was better than nothing. He fetched his phone out, took a deep breath and tapped in the number. A standard voicemail message kicked in, asking him to leave a message. No clues there. He hung up, huffing. He contemplated calling back and leaving a message. But what would he say? It was too risky. If Beth had been the one to call, would she have left a message?

His mind returned to the trip they'd made to her old house that afternoon. It had felt good helping her, and that she'd chosen him rather than Sadie. His cheeks burning despite the chilly air, he forwarded Beth the photo of Mrs Roberts's screen with a quick message to explain. She replied straight away with a shocked face emoji, but nothing more. Jack sighed and carried on through the park.

Before realising it, Jack's feet had carried him to the hospital. It towered above him – a dull hunk of grey squatting between the grand red-bricked Victorian buildings. Jack stared up at the imposing entrance, then he messaged Beth again. *At the hospital. Going to try and see Fabien. Want me to wait for you?*

This time she sent a proper reply. *Cathy's asked me to babysit. Let me know how it goes.*

So Jack was on his own. He pocketed his phone, climbed the main steps and went into the entrance. His foggy brain struggled to make sense of the jumble of signs on the walls pointing in every direction.

"Can I help you?" said a kindly voice. He swung round and was met by a grey-haired man wearing a badge saying, "Helper. Ask me anything."

"I'm looking for the ICU," he said.

"How old is the patient?" asked the helper.

"Thirteen."

"You'll be looking for the paediatric ICU on the second floor." The helper peered at Jack over his half-moon glasses. "I think they've got a family only rule. Are you family?"

"Uh, yes, cousin," said Jack, flinching inwardly at the lie.

The man studied him for a moment and then said, "I'll take you up. This place is a bit of a maze. It's easy to get lost."

They took the lift, the helper keeping up a stream of one-sided chat about who knew what. Jack barely registered his surroundings. Instead, a stream of questions ran on a loop through his mind. Would he be allowed to see Fabien? Would Fabien be battered and bruised? Would he still look like Fabien?

Once on the second floor, Jack followed the helper along endless corridors, twisting this way and that, until they finally reached the entrance to the ICU. The man picked up the entryphone, asked Jack his name and who he was visiting, and relayed the information to the person on the other end of the phone.

The helper hung up. "Fabien's in a stable condition, but has been sedated. He's in room one. Do you want me to come with you? It can be quite upsetting seeing someone in ICU."

Jack shook his head. "I'll be all right," he said, although he was very tempted to turn back and quit this dismal place. The smell of chemicals and something unfamiliar but indescribably bad caught at the back of his throat.

"Use the alcohol gel before you go in." The man pointed to a container fixed to the wall by the door. Jack's fingers trembled as he held them under the nozzle. "Wait here until they let you in. You'll need to speak to the nurse at the desk. I hope your cousin's okay." With a nod of encouragement, the helper left.

Moments later the door clicked open and Jack was inside. The nurses' station lay in front of him. Jack licked his lips, wishing he'd bought a drink at the kiosk they'd passed downstairs. He approached the desk. A nurse was on the phone and tapping at a keyboard at the same time. She looked up at him, mouthed *Be with you in a minute* and gestured towards some hard plastic seats. Jack nodded and backed away. Other nurses and staff members hurried to and fro. A cleaner was mopping the floor with slow, deliberate swipes. Jack hesitated, unsure what to do. *What if the nurse asks for proof that I'm family?* Jack started to feel the first stirrings of panic. He wanted to see Fabien. He had to see him. It was agony not knowing how he really was.

The helper had said Fabien was in room one. Jack glanced around – room one was to the left of the nurses' station. The nurse at the desk was still on the phone, everybody else was busy – Jack inched towards the room.

The sliding door to room one hissed open and the first thing Jack noticed were the two large beds against opposite walls. The person to the left had a tube coming out of his throat which was attached to a machine making a whooshing noise as it pushed and sucked air into and out of his lungs. It wasn't Fabien. Jack took a shaky gulp and turned towards the other bed, steeling himself for what he might find. More machines beeped in time with flashing red and green lights on the displays. Get Well Soon cards were taped on the wall behind them.

Jack crept nearer, trying to steady his breathing, then dragged his gaze towards the bedhead. Fabien was propped up on a mound of pillows. He looked so small in the massive adult-sized bed. So pale and motionless. Dressings covered the left side of his face, and a thin tube, stuck onto his cheek with a bit of white tape, entered his nose. Another in his arm led to a bag of fluid hanging on a stand next to him. His eyes were closed, his chest rising softly up and down as he breathed. He didn't have one of those tubes in his throat. That had to be a good thing. Right?

Jack grabbed the back of a plastic chair placed by the bed, clasping so hard his knuckles went white. Seeing Fabien lying there made everything more real, more horrific, more his fault. He lowered his gaze and stared at his hands, willing them to relax their grip.

He moved nearer the bed and cleared his throat, wishing for the second time he had a drink with him. "Hi, it's Jack. Jack Phillips." *Whoa, I sound like an idiot.* "Look, this is all my fault. I should have protected you from Kai. I'm going to make it up to you, I promise." He took a deep breath. "One way or another."

"Hello."

He spun round, his heart skipping a beat. A small woman with a pointed bird-like face stood in the doorway, a holdall clutched in her arms.

"I'm Fabien's mum, Viola." Jack had never been to Fabien's home, so he hadn't met his parents, although Fabien talked about them loads. The woman stepped into the room, put the bag on the floor and shrugged out of her coat, placing it on the chair. She gazed at him with exhausted, hollow eyes. "You must be—?"

"Jack." Had she heard what he had said about the accident being his fault? His armpits prickled with sweat. *Hold it together*, he willed himself. "From school."

"I'm surprised they let you in here." She didn't sound cross. "It's nice to meet you at last, Jack. Shame it isn't in better circumstances." She rubbed a hand over her face. "Fabien's talked about you."

"How is he?" Jack's words rushed out in relief. She wouldn't have been so nice if she'd overheard his jabbering.

"He's being well looked after. I wish I knew what happened. No one seems to be able to tell me anything, not even the police." She sighed heavily, pushing a wisp of hair away from her eyes. "Were you the one with him when he fell?"

"No." Jack started backing away from the bed towards the door. "Sorry, I've gotta go . . ."

"Of course. Well, thank you for coming. I'll tell him you were here when he wakes up." She was talking as if Fabien was simply taking an afternoon nap. A tired smile appeared on her lips, then vanished as her eyes flitted between Jack and Fabien. Jack edged into the corridor. She followed, as if seeing him out after a visit to her home. "Will you come again? I'll let the nurses know."

The screech of an alarm drowned out his answer. A light on the wall outside the room started flashing. Moments later, two nurses with a trolley piled past them into Fabien's room. A medic followed, her white coat flapping behind her like two huge wings. Fabien's mum reeled back, eyes wide, her hand clamped in horror over her open mouth.

A wave of nausea washed over Jack. He tried to move his feet but couldn't. *What had he done?* More people arrived and rushed into the room. Another alarm went off. He got elbowed to one side. A nurse spoke to him. He didn't know if he replied or not. Someone propelled Fabien's mum away from the doorway. "Let's get you a cup of tea," Jack heard as they whisked her away. Then he was ushered away too.

Chapter Eighteen

Nina was on the phone at the reception desk when Jack arrived at The Willows the next afternoon, worse luck. He'd hoped to slip in unnoticed, since he wasn't sure what kind of welcome he'd get.

She held up a hand, clearly ordering him to wait, then turned her back on him and continued with her call. Jack stood by the desk as she droned on and on to someone called William about Malcolm being on a course all day, and a load of other stuff. Jack yawned. He'd had hardly any sleep the previous night, shocked by what he'd witnessed in the ICU. Every time he closed his eyes an image of Fabien dead in the hospital bed swam into his mind, and he'd sat up, dry-mouthed, head pounding. He'd waited thirty tortuous minutes at the hospital before he'd discovered that the emergency had been to do with the boy in the bed opposite, not Fabien.

Fabien was still alive. Unlike the other boy.

The panic of the previous day hadn't totally disappeared. What if it *had* been Fabien who'd died? What then? Jack wished he'd been able to talk to Beth, tell her what had happened and how awful it had been to see the doctors and nurses fighting and failing to save the other boy's life. But Beth hadn't answered his messages. And so far, there was no sign of her at The Willows.

It was then Jack noticed that the door to the key cupboard in the little office beside the reception desk was ajar. Some areas of the building had digital locks, but others still needed physical keys. Malcolm's office was one of them. Jack's mind whirred . . . Malcolm was away for the day, Nina was busy on the phone . . . this was his chance.

The manager seemed to have forgotten Jack's existence. Keeping half an eye on her, he sidled into the small office and made a beeline for the cupboard. Outside, he heard Nina's high-pitched snorts and giggles. He scanned the keys hanging from the hooks, found the furry lion fob marked "Malcolm's office", grabbed it and slipped out of the room.

He was about to sneak off when Nina ended her call. A slight smile hovered on her lips and Jack swore he heard her humming under her breath. She clocked him gazing at her and two pink circles appeared on her cheeks.

"Right, I want a word with you," she started, then broke off abruptly with a loud "Ah, good afternoon" directed at someone behind him. Jack swivelled around, his fingers automatically tightening on the keys in his hoodie pocket, the metal jabbing into his flesh.

His armpits went sticky with sweat as two police officers marched towards the front desk. One officer caught his eye and smiled, then focused her attention on the manager. "Nina Hughes?"

Nina nodded and motioned towards the cubbyhole office. "This way please."

Jack watched Nina and the two officers disappear into the room. The door clunked shut behind them, indistinct mutterings soon coming from inside. Jack turned away, sick to the pit of his stomach. Was Nina pinning the blame for the thefts on him and Beth? Had she gone behind Malcolm's back to call the police? Why else would they be there?

The keys clenched in his fist were a sharp reminder of his plan. With the police sniffing around, things had got more urgent. *Focus, Jack, focus*, he told himself, pulling his shoulders back. He prayed Nina was too distracted to notice the empty hook in the key cupboard.

Minutes later, he was outside Malcolm's office. There were only two keys on the fob and he picked the larger one. "*Grrrrr*" growled the lion fob. Jack desperately tried to find a switch to turn the electronic noise off. There wasn't one. Cursing under his breath, he did his best to muffle the sound with his fingers while rushing to fit the key in the lock. His hand trembled, his panicked breaths coming faster and faster. At any moment he'd hear Nina's angry squawk behind him. *Come on*, he willed himself.

"Let me." A pale hand grasped his own. Jack's gaze skipped sideways, his heartbeat kicking faster. It was only Beth. He exhaled the tension away and let her take the keys. After a couple of twists and turns, the lock gave a satisfying click, and they were in.

"How did you know I was here?" he asked, scanning the room.

"I didn't," Beth said calmly, and handed the keys back to him. "I had the same idea as you – to find out what Mrs Roberts was doing in here. Better hurry up, Nina's always prowling around. I'll keep watch while you search."

Jack picked his way between the mounds of stuff on the floor, thinking hard as he did so. If Mrs Roberts was the one stealing stuff from residents, what would she find of use in the office? Maybe she thought they kept money in there? He glanced around the room – no sign of a safe, though it was difficult to see amongst all the mess. And he and Beth had heard Malcolm saying he was short of cash. If that was true, he probably didn't have money in his office. Mrs Harper seemed convinced the cleaner, Ray, was the thief . . . were Mrs Roberts and Kai in on it with him? But none of that explained why Mrs Roberts had been in Malcolm's office.

Jack had to concentrate on what they *did* know. Mrs Roberts was pretending to be deaf, plus she had mysterious phone calls and a strange visitor to her home. And while in Malcolm's office, she had uncovered something important enough to take photos of.

Jack saw a laptop lying on top of a metal filing cabinet. He pulled it down onto the desk, trying not to cough at the dislodged cloud of dust. Nothing happened when he pressed the on button, and he couldn't see a power cable anywhere. He turned his attention to the filing cabinet, remembering the metallic rattling he'd heard when Mrs Roberts was there. It was locked, but the smaller key sorted out that problem. He glanced at the crammed drawer he'd pulled out and his heart sank. Going through all this would be an impossible task.

"Found anything?" whispered Beth from her post by the door.

"Wait." Jack spotted something brown on top of the cabinet. He picked it up and showed it to Beth. It was a roll of parcel tape. "It's the same as the tape on the packet from the roof."

Beth raised an eyebrow. "A roll of parcel tape doesn't prove a thing."

Jack groaned, turning again to face the chaos of the office. "I don't know what to look for. It's hopeless."

"Mrs Roberts would have been in a rush," said Beth. "She'd start with easy-to-search places." Beth was right. What Mrs Roberts found wasn't in a file on Malcolm's dead computer, nor stuck in an over-stuffed cabinet . . .

Jack started searching the room. Where *would* the old woman have looked first? His gaze fell upon a messy stack of papers on the desk with a dirty mug balancing on top. Jack scooped the papers up, keeping an ear open for sounds outside, and a large, thin cardboard folder slipped from the pile onto the floor. On the front someone had written "Confidential".

"Open it," said Beth.

Jack joined her by the door, took a deep breath and opened the flap. He pulled out two sheets of paper and handed one to Beth. Each page was divided into columns with a handwritten list of names on the left, followed by a column headed "Apartment Number". A third column had the title "Insurance Company" and a fourth said

"Date". But it was the two columns on the right which made his heart miss a beat as he read:

Five-stone diamond ring – £4,000?

Ruby drop earrings – £250?

24-carat yellow-gold chain – £2,500?

Ladies Omega watch – £1,500?

The list went on.

"It's a list of residents' valuables," said Beth. "But why would Malcolm have this? It doesn't make sense. Everyone insures their own belongings. Look." She pointed at the "Insurance Company" column. "Mrs Harper uses SwiftSafe, Mr Garibaldi uses Safe and Secure, Dr Bellini has Insure Better . . . It's nothing to do with Malcolm, so why does he have this list? Unless . . ."

A horrible taste rose in Jack's mouth. "Unless he's involved in the thefts too," he finished. "But that doesn't explain Mrs Roberts's part in this." Jack took the page back from Beth and returned to the desk. "It feels as if there are too many suspects."

"I can't believe Malcolm's in on it. He loves the people here. He's always going on about it being a great community," said Beth. "If Mrs Roberts discovered this list, she'd know which apartments Jolly or Ray needed to search to get their hands on valuables."

Jack thought again of the flashes he'd seen through the frosted glass. Something didn't add up. "I only saw her in here yesterday. Fabien says the stealing's been going on for weeks."

"She's just found the list, so what? Maybe she got lucky before."

"Maybe." Jack wasn't convinced.

"Then Kai forced Fabien to do the risky work of getting the stuff away from the home. Clever," Beth continued.

But Mrs Roberts hadn't been clever enough not to be seen by Jack coming out of Malcolm's office, he thought.

"Perhaps Malcolm tells Jolly or Ray which residents have valuables, and they pay him money for his trouble," said Beth, and she took another peek into the corridor.

"And Mrs Roberts? What's her involvement? We're going round in circles with this." Jack's pulse quickened – they must have been in the office for ages. The longer they were there, the more likely Nina would discover them. He took out his phone to check the time and the Write a Will with Bill business card that Mr Garibaldi had given him dropped onto the desk. Jack left it there while he hurried to switch the flash of his phone off – the last thing he wanted was to alert anyone to them being in the office, as Mrs Roberts had done. His hand was trembling as he took photos of the lists. He didn't even check if the images were blurry, scooping up the pages, sliding them back into the folder and shoving it back in between the pile of papers. He went to put the business card back in his pocket, and the phone number caught his eye. Something clicked in his mind. The number started with 0141 111 . . . Where had he seen that number before?

"Jack!" said Beth, her hand on the door knob ready to make a run for it. "Come on!"

"Wait a sec!" Jack grabbed his phone again and scrolled through the gallery until he found the photo he'd taken of Mrs Roberts's call log. And there it was. The same number. Mrs Roberts had called Mr "Write a Will with Bill". It didn't have to be dodgy, Jack told himself. She might have wanted to make a will – she had to be old enough to need one. But that thought didn't get rid of Jack's doubts.

A door slammed somewhere outside. They had to get a move on. The puzzle of Bill would have to wait till later. Grabbing the keys, Jack cast one last look around the room, then joined Beth in the corridor, locking the door behind them. There was no one around, but Jack only allowed himself the luxury of a relieved sigh once they'd put some distance between themselves and Malcolm's office.

Chapter Nineteen

As they rushed away, Jack realised he hadn't had the chance to tell Beth about the police officers' arrival. Luckily, neither Nina nor the officers were around when Jack and Beth got back to the reception. Beth went straight outside, while he slipped into the cubbyhole office and hung the lion fob back on its hook.

"What are you doing?"

Jack sprang back from the key cupboard. Nina was in the doorway, her eyebrows knotted into an angry frown. "I-I was looking for you."

"You have no business in my office," she hissed, crimson blotches appearing on her neck. "No business at all."

"S-Sorry," he stuttered. "I wanted to ask if you'd take a better photo of me for my pass."

"Out," Nina said. Jack didn't hesitate. He squeezed past her bulky frame and into the hall. "You won't be needing your pass any longer. Sneaking about like that, going into places you shouldn't. Stealing stuff, no doubt."

"I'm not a thief," said Jack. "I—"

Beth bounded back in from the lobby. "What's the hold-up?" She stopped dead on seeing Nina.

Nina ignored Beth and glared at Jack. "I'll be telling the police about this. I've already given them your details. They'll be visiting you for sure."

"I haven't stolen anything," said Jack.

"Jack's not a thief!" said Beth.

"Tell that to the officers. In the meantime, you're banned from here. Give me your pass." Nina extended a hand and beckoned with her fingers. "And yours too," she said to Beth.

Beth dumped hers on the reception desk, her face stony. Jack did the same.

"Come on, Jack. We'll talk to Malcolm. He won't like this." Beth grabbed his sleeve and started pulling him towards the lobby.

"Don't think Malcolm will help you!" screeched Nina. "He'll agree with me."

They legged it through the lobby, out of the main doors and into the open. Sharp air blasted Jack's face, making his eyes sting, but he took great gulps of it, attempting to calm himself. Nina's accusation rang loud in his ears.

Beth was seething, wheeling round to him as soon as they cleared the steps at the entrance. "How dare she accuse you? I bet loads of staff go in her stupid office without permission."

"Trouble is, I'm only a volunteer, aren't I?"

"Still, what happened to innocent till proven guilty?"

Jack shrugged. It didn't matter what Beth thought. Nina was the one in charge and she'd banned them. Misery wrapped around him like a sopping wet towel. How had things got so bad? How were they going to find the real thieves if they'd been banned from the building? How would Jack check on Mr G? How would he get to talk to Mr G about Fabien?

The setting sun was almost invisible behind a towering bank of grey autumnal clouds, and the little garden lamps sunk in the flower beds edging the car park pinged into life. They splashed a faint ashy glow on the tarmac at their feet. As Jack and Beth passed the fountain, he shivered. The gaping mouths of the stone fish were lit up a sinister ghostly grey too.

They moved onto the street and went over again what they'd already found out: Mrs Harper's missing watch and her blaming the cleaner, Jolly's suspicious behaviour, Mrs Roberts's search of Malcolm's office and the lists of valuables they'd stumbled across in there.

"Mrs Roberts is either working with someone else, maybe the cleaner or Jolly, or it's just her and Kai," Beth said. "It's obvious she's not an innocent old lady."

"But it all seems too . . ."

"Too what?"

"Unlikely," finished Jack as they reached the traffic lights at the end of the street. They both took a step back while a bus trundled past, splashing the pavement with dirty rainwater from the gutter.

"If Mrs Roberts is a thief, she's not very good at it. Look at these." He got out his phone to show Beth the photos he'd taken, as the pedestrian lights turned green and they set off again.

She gave them a dismissive glance. "Nice one. I think you've found your perfect job – photographer."

"You're missing the point. I took these without the flash. Only an idiot would use the flash and risk getting caught."

"So?"

"Mrs Roberts used the flash."

"She made a mistake." Impatience flitted across Beth's face. "What's the problem? It wasn't long ago that you thought she was a spy or something."

True. He had thought Mrs Roberts was suspicious – she always seemed to be hanging around, watching him, and turning up in unlikely places when he was searching for Dad. But this was different, wasn't it? She was behaving oddly, he couldn't deny it. But something was off about it all. "How much has Cathy told you about Malcolm?" Jack asked. "Because he knows everything about the people living there. *Everything*. He's in the perfect position to—"

"Malcolm wouldn't do anything to hurt people there," Beth cut him off, but Jack heard a flicker of doubt in her voice. "Look how he acts with the residents. He loves them."

Jack stayed silent, his eyes boring holes in the pavement at his feet. They continued walking, dodging past a load of workers spilling out of an office.

"Besides," she carried on. "It's way too obvious."

"Malcom's got the opportunity to do the stealing – he's always in and out of people's apartments."

"So is the cleaner," Beth reminded him.

"Want a drink?" Jack gestured towards the welcoming warm light of a nearby café. The smell of freshly baked chocolate brownies wafted out of the open door, making Jack's taste buds go into overdrive. "I'll pay."

Happily Beth said yes, and a couple of minutes later they were sitting at a window table looking out onto the dark, rain-splattered street, nursing mugs of steaming hot chocolate.

Beth blew on the liquid in her mug. "Did you get to see Fabien last night?"

A lump lodged in Jack's throat as he thought back to his shocking visit to the hospital. "Yeah," he finally muttered. "He was lying there like a vegetable." Then he told her about meeting Fabien's mum and the emergency to do with the other boy.

Beth's eyes got wider and wider. "What a nightmare! It must have been terrible for you. And poor Fabien."

"Yeah, it was . . . bad." Jack couldn't think of the right words to describe his horror at seeing Fabien so sick. He took a deep breath. "There's something else you should know – Nina called the police."

"What?" Beth's eyebrows shot up under her fringe. "Since when?"

"I didn't have time to tell you, but before you turned up today, two officers were there talking to Nina. Say she tells them I'm responsible for the thefts *and* Fabien's accident? If he doesn't wake up and tell the truth, I could be accused of attempted murder."

"That's not going to happen," said Beth. "But we've got to sort this whole thing out. Let's go over the facts again."

"Maybe Malcolm's broke, or in debt . . ." said Jack, as Beth took a knife to a brownie and handed him half. "We heard him on the phone talking about money problems. And he didn't want to call the police, it was Nina. If Malcolm's got something to hide, he could be keeping it secret from Nina too. Say he's the criminal mastermind? The evidence is there."

"But if Mrs Roberts and Malcolm are working together, why was she snooping in his office? It doesn't make sense . . ."

"None of it makes sense," admitted Jack with a huff. Deep down, he didn't know what to believe. Malcolm seemed friendly and kind. He cracked jokes with the residents, and he might have been disorganised, but people liked him. "Don't forget, Malcolm has that list of valuables. The question is: why?"

Suddenly Beth dumped the rest of her brownie back on the plate and seized Jack's phone.

"Hey, what are you doing?"

"Where are those photos you took in Malcolm's office?"

"Here." He snatched the phone back, scrolled through the gallery and showed her the first photo.

"Zoom in." She gestured to the picture of the list. "I want to see the names."

Jack did as he was told, feeling a bit annoyed at her bossing him about.

"Aha, thought so!" Beth said as she looked at the close-up image.

Jack glanced at her, puzzled.

She pointed at the screen. "What do you see?"

He shrugged. "A list of apartment owners."

"Yeah," she said impatiently. "But look at that one." She pointed at the top of the list of valuables.

"Mrs Joyliffe. So what?"

"You're so slow," she said. "What's the number of her apartment?"

Jack gave an irritated sigh and glanced at the photo again. "Two . . ."

"Which apartment did you see the security guard coming out of?"

"Number two, which is Mrs Joyli . . . Ah!" Jack finally understood what she was getting at. When he'd scanned the photo earlier, he hadn't taken much notice of the names, just the valuables. "Jolly's real name could be Joyliffe, not Jolly! They might be related!"

"Exactly, that's what I think," Beth replied. "Jolly's a nickname. A good one since he's pretty much the opposite. It would be easy to check if Nina hadn't banned us from The Willows." She huffed out, the air rippling her fringe. "I've never taken any notice of Jolly's pass, but maybe his real name's on it. That's why you saw him coming out of her apartment. She's his mum, or sister, or another relative."

"He looked guilty though," said Jack. He felt silly not to have thought of that reason for Jolly being in the apartment. "And no one was at home."

"Think about it. He should be working. Instead, he sneaks in there to have a break or coffee or watch TV, even if no one's in. Who would know? The question is, would Jolly steal from his own mum? Do we knock him off our list of suspects?"

Jack thought hard. "I suppose he moves right to the bottom of the list."

"There's something else we've forgotten – Kai's uncle. Remember, that wasn't Malcolm we heard in Kai's flat. So assuming it wasn't Jolly, and we know it wasn't Mrs Roberts, who's left?"

"Ray," said Jack triumphantly. "The cleaner."

Chapter Twenty

"What do you want?" said the squatter.

It was late Sunday afternoon. A quick trip, Beth had told Jack, then they'd find a way into The Willows to investigate the cleaner. Conchita had told Beth that Ray worked until seven in the evening, so they had time. Jack would rather have gone straight to The Willows – he was the one, after all, that was being accused of the thefts. He needed answers, and fast. But Beth had asked for his help. There was no way he'd let her down.

That was how they came to be standing outside Beth's old house again, in the shadow of a tree, craning up to look at a first-floor window. A girl had stuck her head out as soon as they'd walked up the path. A few years older than Jack and Beth, her face was full of distrust.

"We're not here to bother you," said Beth. "We need your help."

The girl regarded them for a moment, not saying anything, then withdrew her head. Jack and Beth exchanged glances, wondering what to do. But a minute later, the girl came around the side of the house. Her face was grimy and her hair hung in matted strands down to her shoulders. Her jeans were ripped with huge holes in the knees and she was wearing a padded jacket far too big for her, and greying sneakers. As she got nearer, Jack saw she was carrying a piece of wood with a big nail sticking out of it. It was hanging limply at her side, but an icy chill gripped Jack's insides.

"This is my place," said the girl, advancing a step further.

Beth backed off, putting her hands up, palms out. "We don't want any trouble."

"You were here the other day." The girl glanced warily from Beth to Jack and rested one end of the plank on the ground, leaning on the other like a crutch.

"Yes," said Beth. Jack flicked a look at her – she sounded so calm. "I used to live here."

"I live here now."

"It's not yours. You're squatting," said Beth coolly. "How come?"

The girl rubbed a dirty hand across her brow as if she'd got a sudden ache there. "Not that it's any of your business, but my dad chucked me out six months ago. I

146

saw this place was empty so . . . I'm not doing any harm. Got to live somewhere."

"You busted the lock," said Jack.

The girl's gaze shifted to him. "Easy to fix."

Beth looked at the shuttered windows. "What happened to the people who used to live here?"

"How would I know? I'm just the homeless girl who squats," she said, doing air quotes when she said "squats". Then, seeming to regret her hostile tone, she added, "It's probably been repossessed. The bank will own it now. That's what happened to my dad's place when he didn't pay the mortgage. Anyway, what do you want?"

"I need to go inside."

The girl tilted her head in a question. "Why?"

Jack pulled Beth to one side and whispered out of the corner of his mouth, "This is madness. How do you know we can trust her?"

"We don't, but I have to take a chance." Beth shook his hand off and fished the chain out from the neck of her sweater, turning back to the strange girl. "My parents left me this key. I want to check if it opens a cupboard or drawer in the house."

"And if I let you?" In the half-light the girl's features looked pointed like a ferret's.

Beth rummaged in her bag and brought out her purse. She showed the girl two ten-pound notes. "This is all I have. It's from the last of my birthday money. Take it."

The girl was silent for a second, then grabbed the money and jerked her head for them to go inside. They sidled past her, Jack keeping his eyes pinned on the girl *and* the plank of wood. Beth might have been happy to trust the squatter, but he wasn't. On his way through the garden he grabbed a stick, just in case . . .

Once inside the house Beth led the way up the stairs, throwing open the door to the first room at the top.

"This was Mum and Dad's bedroom," she said, her voice trembling. The rude girl pushed past, telling them to wait, and disappeared inside. Seconds later she reappeared, without the plank but with a torch. She beckoned them in with the beam.

"Their bed used to go against that wall." Beth pointed opposite the window to where a sleeping bag was heaped on top of a mattress of newspapers and cardboard. There were bits of cardboard taped at the windows too.

"I can't sleep with the lights from the street," explained the girl, when she saw Jack staring at them. All the same, she folded a corner of the card away from the glass, so a weak stream of orange street light filtered across the floorboards.

The room was freezing. If it had been light enough, Jack was sure he'd see his breath coming from his mouth. His gaze swept towards the fire grate, which was depressingly empty, but next to it was an alcove with a tall cupboard. Beth was already pulling open the doors. She gave an excited squeal. "Look at this."

The top of the cupboard had a rail for hanging clothes. Underneath there were three smallish drawers, the top one of which had a tiny keyhole. The girl came closer.

"Go on then," she said. "What are you waiting for?"

Beth knelt and with shaky hands inserted her key. It fitted. With an easy twist, she unlocked the drawer, pulled it open and patted inside, eventually taking it out, turning it upside down and banging the base.

"Nothing," Beth huffed, sitting back on her heels.

"Wait," said the girl, and she pushed them both aside. "Sometimes things can get trapped . . ." She stuck her hand into the hole where the drawer had been and rummaged around. "Which would explain –" more rummaging – "why this got left behind." With a triumphant flourish, she produced a small square cardboard box. Beth held her hand out for it, but the girl jerked it out of her reach and flicked the lid off. "Ugh, it's a lump of old metal. Worthless." She thrust the box into Beth's hands.

"What *is* that?" Jack peered over Beth's shoulder at the weirdly shaped lump of metal about the size of a ten-pence coin that nestled on tissue paper at the bottom of the box.

Clearly still curious, the girl held the torch up, while Beth and Jack huddled together to examine it. The object was a dirty-silver colour. And it wasn't just a formless lump. It had a definite shape – almost pointed at the bottom, becoming fatter towards the middle, then narrowing again at the top where there was a metal loop. A pattern of etched lines covered the surface. The fat end had what looked like tiny engraved pipes or tubes leading from the top.

"Give me that a sec," said Beth, grabbing the torch from the girl and shining it on the lump. "It's an anatomical heart. See, here's the pulmonary vein, and the superior vena cava. And here are the chambers, too. It's beautiful."

Jack didn't have a clue what Beth was talking about, but standing around in the dark, cold room with the girl watching them was giving him the heebie-jeebies. "You've got it, so let's go."

"Wait," whispered Beth. She handed the torch to Jack and grasped the heart between her fingers. "Look, it's got a hinge . . ." Jack craned over her shoulder, shining the torch on her hand. She prised the two sides of the heart apart with her nails. Inside lay a tiny roll of paper. With trembling fingers, Beth hooked it out. "It's a message!"

On it, in tiny writing, were the words: "To my budding doctor, happy 12th birthday, love always, Mum and Dad xxx".

"They must have been planning to give it to me on my birthday, before they died." Beth's voice wobbled. "It's been here all that time!"

The girl, obviously disappointed that it wasn't anything more exciting than a piece of paper, had gone to sit on her sleeping bag in the corner, and was rolling a cigarette.

"Thanks for your help," said Beth, turning towards her.

The girl shrugged and lay on her back on her makeshift bed. "You know the way out." She turned from them and huddled deeper into her sleeping bag.

Jack had to practically drag Beth out of the house and all the way to the bus stop. The only thing she had eyes for was the locket and the tiny message in her hand.

As they waited for the bus, Jack's phone rang. It was Auntie Lil. She sounded hassled. "Where are you?" she asked.

"On my way to The Willows."

"The police called. They want to see you at the station. Something about thefts at the home. And they want to talk to you about Fabien's fall. What's it all about, Jack? What have you got yourself into?"

An icy fist grabbed at Jack's heart. "It's nothing, Auntie Lil. A mix-up, that's all."

Auntie Lil didn't sound reassured. "What will your mum say about this?"

"Please don't mention it to her. She'll only get worried," pleaded Jack, imagining Mum rushing home after finding out her only son was being held by the police. "It's all a big mistake."

"The police want us to go down there tomorrow afternoon. Then you'll have to tell your mum, Jack. She needs to know." Jack heard her sigh down the phone line. "Well, I'll leave some dinner for you. I've got a splitting headache, so I'm off to bed. Make sure you're not back late tonight."

Jack agreed miserably, then ended the call. The bus pulled up and he hurried to join Beth on-board. They *had* to prove Ray was the criminal, not Jack, and fast. The evidence was stacking up against Jack like newly laid bricks in a wall – the thefts began about the time he'd started at The Willows; Malcolm had found him wandering the corridors of the building when Mrs Harper had reported her watch missing; Nina had spotted him sneaking out of the cubbyhole office. Even the chef had caught him hiding in the kitchen. And all that without even mentioning Fabien's so-called accident. Jack looked very guilty. He was even starting to feel guilty! Maybe he'd be arrested tomorrow. He imagined being thrown into a cell with a hard bench for a bed and cockroaches for company. What would Mum say? And Dad? How could he tell the police what was really going on? He'd drop Fabien right in it. Jack was the prime suspect, and right then it felt as if there was absolutely nothing he could do about it.

Chapter Twenty-One

The bus dropped them near The Willows, but as they were banned, they could hardly stroll through the main entrance. Besides, Jolly locked the doors at some point in the evening and they didn't know the code to get in. Their choice was either to scale the walls of the building like monkeys (not very tempting since the chances of being spotted by someone in the building or from the street were high) or go via the rooftops and in through the attic window Fabien used. The second option won, of course.

Jack found a secluded alleyway and stopped by a large roller door belonging to some kind of car workshop, judging by the signs fixed to the wall. It was dark and cold. Beth wrapped her scarf more tightly around her neck as gusts of frosty air whistled between the tall buildings either side of the alleyway. The weather matched Jack's mood.

"We should have come earlier instead of going to your old house," he grumped, rubbing his icy hands together. "Now it's really dark."

"We didn't know then that the police were on to you," Beth pointed out.

He glared at her. "You're talking as if I'm the one who did it!"

"Sorry, that came out wrong."

"It'd be different if they were pointing the finger at *you*." Jack's words were out before he could stop them.

"Well, you didn't have to go with me, did you?" she said sharply.

Jack had no answer to that. She was right, after all. But didn't she realise how much trouble he was in? He shook his shoulders back and huffed out, the air from his mouth warm against his icy lips. Using the brackets of a drainpipe as footholds, he climbed the brick wall of the workshop, reaching the top without a problem. He hissed down to Beth to hurry up.

Tube railings bordered the sloping metal roof. In one easy move, he grabbed the top bar with both hands and used it to propel his legs and torso over, his feet finding the surface on the other side. Once safe, he paused, waiting for Beth to catch up. Everything was going well.

The workshop was a short way from the labyrinth of older pitched rooftops and the attic window of The Willows. It was a long time since Jack had been on top of the workshop, but the warehouse roof he normally used was too far away. He avoided metal panelled roofs if he could, because there was little shade and the panels corroded with age. Shade wasn't a problem right then, but the roof was old – very old.

He stepped away from the railing to survey the dark expanse of roofing. The plain of panels stretched away from him into the oncoming dimness. But something about the scene was off. Something that took his brain a second to compute.

"Where are the skylights?" asked Beth from somewhere behind, voicing the same thought a moment before him. That was what was wrong. He'd been expecting to see the series of dirty, plastic windows set into the metal panels which, during the day, allowed sunlight to stream into the workshop below. In the twilight, it was easier to see the brittle skylights and avoid them, but in the darkness, the roof was a shadowy, grubby plateau with nothing to distinguish one part from another.

A chill raced down his spine. He grabbed his phone from his pocket and shone its torch along the roof. The beam wasn't powerful enough to light up more than a metre or so in front of them. Not only did they have corroded metal to worry about, but one wrong step on a hidden, flimsy skylight and they'd plunge eight metres into the workshop below. What a numbskull! Why hadn't he picked a different route? What was his back-up plan? There was no back-up plan. He'd cocked up, big time.

"Shall we come back at sunrise?" said Beth. "We'll be able to see what we're doing then."

Jack's mind was running riot. It was tempting to forget the whole thing – to go home and bury his head under the duvet. But that wouldn't solve anything. He needed answers, and he needed them quickly. Besides, he would never get to sleep with all the stuff churning in his head. He glanced at his watch. It was after six. "Old people get up early, don't they? There'll be more people about, more chance of being discovered. And we don't know if Ray will be there early in the morning."

"What about finding another way?"

"No time. The cleaner will have gone. This could be our only chance to catch Ray in the act." Jack looked at Beth, his torch illuminating her black-lined eyes and ashy cheeks. She looked like a phantom. "I'm going to carry on. You go back if you want. It's going to be tough."

"Don't be an idiot," she said, giving him a forced grin, her teeth glinting in the beam of light. "You can't fall to your death alone."

"Thanks for the vote of confidence," he muttered, but he was secretly pleased that she was coming with him. He was more scared now than ever.

The old rooftops started just beyond the workshop roof. He pocketed his phone, not able to hold it and crawl at the same time. "We'll have to do this bit on all fours," he called, and dropped to his knees.

Ridges and grooves covered the panels, which sloped upwards from the guttering. Step by shaky step, they crawled along the metal, keeping near the relative safety of the railings. Then Jack switched direction, heading up the gentle incline to the ridge. The further away from the street they moved, the darker the sky became. Jack blinked and rubbed his eyes, as if that would help him see better.

As the skylights were spaced out and in rows, all they had to do was find the gap between the rows. Easy. Or was it? Where did the row start? Jack peered into the gloom. It was impossible to tell which part of the roof had a skylight and which didn't.

Creak, creak. The old panels shifted underneath them as they crawled along. Every second shuffle, Jack stopped and prodded the panels with his hands, feeling for a rim or ledge, or anything that might mark a skylight. He and Beth didn't talk much. He was concentrating hard, and he guessed she was too. Now and then, she bumped his trainer with a hand and he could hear her breathing noisily through her mouth. It was the only way to tell that she was still behind him. After a few more minutes of crawling they reached the roof ridge, and still on hands and knees, started down the other side.

There was a loud metallic screech. CRACK! Something gave way under him. His right leg dropped through the roof, pain blazing through his knee. He bit his top lip hard, stifling a scream.

"Jack?" A light from Beth's phone torch shone in his eyes as her face loomed large.

"Aargh!" he said in response, and tried to free his leg. Each movement was like a nail being hammered into his kneecap.

Putting her phone down, Beth wrapped her arms around his chest from behind to steady him as he tried to pull his leg out of the hole. White-hot pain seared through his knee and down his calf. Bile rose in his throat and he retched as his leg came free and he drew it up onto the roof. "How bad is it?" he croaked.

"Let me check," she said, eyeing his leg with worry. Jack steeled himself to take a look. A large tear stretched across the knee of his jeans, and blood seeped through the thick fabric, staining it dark. Beth took her water bottle out of her backpack – he tried not to scream as the cold water hit the wound. In contrast, his cheeks were fiery-hot. Beth wrapped her scarf tightly around the wound. "It's not deep, but with your skin . . ."

"I'll live," he said shakily, at the same time picturing infected yellow pus oozing from the fleshy part of his knee. The thought made him gag again.

"Can you move?" said Beth, taking hold of his arm. He nodded. *Be brave, Jack*, he told himself. They half-crawled, half-shuffled down the metal roof. Relief flooded Jack's veins when they reached the first of the older rooftops and more familiar territory. He prayed the worst was over.

Up, down, up, down, they crossed the Victorian tiles, concentrating on the few metres in front of them. It was hard not to be anxious about his knee – it throbbed with each step – and even harder not to wish that they'd taken their chances in scaling the walls of The Willows.

It was pitch-black by the time they arrived exhausted on the roof of The Willows. Beth insisted they stop for a quick rest and to check Jack's knee – it had stopped bleeding, thankfully, and the pain wasn't so terrible – then they made for the attic window, which was open a crack. Jack slid his fingers between the sill and frame and jerked the window upwards. The gap was tight, but there was enough space to squeeze his body through. Beth followed.

"This way," she whispered, pointing with her phone torch to a route between the packing crates, stacked higgledy-piggledy. Trying to calm his galloping heart, he picked his way across the room. Boxes, bags, old furniture, broken beds, old mattresses and wheelchairs were piled against the walls and in dusty corners, but someone had cleared a passageway from the window to the door. Footprints, presumably Fabien's, marked the dirty floorboards.

The door was unlocked. There were no windows in the attic corridors and the air smelt stale and of mouldy carpet, but a light clicked on automatically as they moved, so Beth put her phone away. Jack prayed that nobody was around to notice that the light was on. The ceilings were low and sloped, the walls covered in chipped, flaky paint. They tiptoed past closed doors, pausing at every creak and thud.

Beth was as jittery as he was. "What's that?" she squeaked, on hearing a loud knocking noise.

"Water in the pipes," he replied, though he wasn't at all sure.

But the attic floor appeared deserted, and they soon came across a narrow flight of stairs leading down. Jack's leg throbbed and he toyed with the idea of taking the lift from the second floor, but quickly dismissed that thought. Trapped in a metal box with no escape? Bad idea.

Before they exited into the corridor on the first floor, they paused for another breather.

"I'll see if I can find out for sure what Jolly's surname is," said Beth. "You find the cleaner. Meet you back here in fifteen minutes?"

Jack nodded, took a deep breath and pushed open the fire door at the bottom of the staircase.

Chapter Twenty-Two

They parted ways in the first-floor corridor. Jack wanted to check on Mr Garibaldi, but first he had to locate the cleaner and find the proof he so desperately needed. Jack still had a niggling doubt – why would Ray not remove the stolen items himself? But he quashed that thought. There'd be time to sort out the whys later.

Ray's cleaning cart was parked in the corridor to the right of the galleried landing. This was Jack's chance. After checking the cleaner wasn't around – all was quiet – Jack hurried that way. A large yellow waste sack was attached to the handle. Jack glanced inside, scrunching up his nose. Could that be where Ray hid what he stole? It looked as if it just contained rubbish, but without sticking his hand in, there was no way of knowing for sure. Delaying that moment, he examined the rest of the cart. There were two shelves of cleaning products, a holder for a mop and broom, and a platform with a bucket on it. First, he inspected the spray bottles and containers of cleaning stuff. Nothing strange about those, and nothing hidden between them. The bucket was empty too. He was about to pluck up courage to examine the contents of the yellow sack when a door opened further down the corridor. Jack dived into a nearby alcove and crouched behind a huge plant on a pedestal, peering out between the leaves. Ray came out with a black bin liner in one hand and dragging the vacuum cleaner behind him with the other.

Jack inhaled sharply – the bin liner was like the one that had been stuffed between the chimney pots. *Get real,* he told to himself. *All bin liners look the same. There's nothing unusual about a cleaner having one, nothing at all. It doesn't prove anything.* Still, Jack carried on watching. The cleaner deposited the contents of the bin liner into the yellow sack, dumped the bin liner on top of the cleaning stuff and heaved the vacuum cleaner onto the platform next to the bucket. Jack had to search that yellow sack. Ray started whistling as he pushed the cart further along, then his two-way radio crackled into life.

"Ray? *Bzzzz* . . . Storeroom one . . ."

Ray swore, and grabbed the radio from his belt. "On my way." He hurried off, leaving his cart parked in the corridor.

Adrenaline kicking in, Jack seized his chance. He scooted out from behind the plant and made for the trolley. He peered inside the sack, holding his breath to avoid inhaling. All he could see were wrappers and food packets. There was nothing for it – he rolled up a sleeve, pushed his hand in and rummaged amongst the wet, sticky contents. It was pretty disgusting. Too late, he saw a pair of rubber gloves stuffed beside the bucket.

A suited man appeared at the end of the corridor. In panic, Jack removed his hand, wiped it on his jeans – *yuck* – and ducked back into the alcove. He observed the man, his mind whirring . . . expensive suit, sausage-shaped fingers clamping a sleek black mobile to his ear, silver hair curling over his shirt collar . . . and a sickly sweet aftershave which clawed at Jack's throat. *That smell . . .*

Suit Man had passed his hiding place by the time Jack realised where he remembered it from. This was the man Jack had seen outside Mrs Roberts's flat. Suit Man stopped walking, still in deep conversation, oblivious to Jack half-crouched behind the plant stand. Then he twisted back Jack's way, halting right by his hiding place. Jack could have reached out and touched the man's polished shoes. He tried his best to keep still, but his legs were cramping, and there was nothing he could do to stop his heart drumming against his ribs. Was it as loud as it sounded to him? *Bang, bang, bang, bang . . .*

"Don't worry about Malcolm," Suit Man was saying. "I'm seeing him and Nina later." A pause, then, "You concentrate on the boy . . . word is that he's on the mend . . ."

The boy? Is he talking about Fabien? Jack forced himself to focus on Suit Man. It wasn't only the aftershave Jack recognised. *I've heard that voice before . . .* With pain screaming through his bad knee, Jack shifted, bumping his shoulder against the plant stand as he did so.

"Wait," ordered Suit Man into the phone, and the shoes moved away a few steps. Silence. Jack held his breath, not daring to move again, the thrumming in his chest still impossibly loud.

No sound from the man. *What's going on?* Jack took a quick peek around the stand. Suit Man was staring down the corridor, then he shrugged to himself and gave a noisy exhalation into the phone. "I've got a meeting now – last blasted will I'll be writing. Don't cock things up again." He hung up and sauntered away.

At last Jack could breathe freely. It was only when he stood upright that he saw the dark stain of blood from his leg on the carpet. He wriggled out from his poky hiding place and stretched his back. His mind was buzzing. *Could Suit Man be Kai's uncle?* Jack was now convinced that it was the voice he'd heard in Kai's place. First, the man had appeared at Mrs Roberts's flat, and now wandering the corridors of The Willows. Then it struck Jack – Suit Man had talked about writing a will. So was Suit Man Mr "Write a Will with Bill"? He had to be. And Bill's phone number, the one on the business card, was logged on Mrs Roberts's phone. Jack had forgotten that. Was it all a coincidence? Somehow he doubted it.

With no time left to look for Mr Garibaldi, Jack hurried back to the stairwell to meet Beth with questions whirring around his brain. Were Bill and Mrs Roberts in it together with Kai? Was Malcolm involved too? And Nina? And the boy Bill had talked about had to be Fabien, which meant he was getting better! Jack felt giddy with relief. Everything was still a muddle, but the pieces of the puzzle were falling into place at last. The problem was they had no proof.

Beth was waiting for him when he got to the stairs. "Jolly's real name is definitely Joyliffe. I checked papers in his office."

"Find anything else?"

Beth shook her head. "Unless you count more rolls of brown parcel tape. So we can rule Jolly out."

Jack nodded impatiently, then briefed her on what he'd discovered about Bill.

"Genius!" she said. "It sounds as if Mrs Roberts and Bill are working together. If you're right, Bill finds out what to steal by quizzing people when he makes their wills. He's been coming here for years – they must trust him. It's perfect."

"So Mrs Roberts was in Malcolm's office because . . . ?"

"That bit still doesn't make sense," admitted Beth, as they went up the stairs. "Bill wouldn't need the list. Perhaps it's not important at all. Maybe it's a red herring. You know, a false clue, like in a detective story. Anyway, good work," she said, then stopped dead, causing Jack to cannon into the back of her.

"What's up?" Jack asked.

"If what Bill said was true, Fabien's getting better, but . . ."

"But what?"

"I've had a terrible thought . . ."

"Hang on." Jack hurried them through the corridor to the attic. Once safely inside with the door shut, he faced her. "Spill."

Beth exhaled. "Bill told Kai to deal with the boy. What if Kai goes to the hospital to silence Fabien before he blabs?"

Jack's stomach clenched. Beth was right. Kai could have been on his way to the hospital, while they wasted time talking about fish. Jack's relief that Fabien was getting better was fizzling away fast. His friend was still in danger.

Chapter Twenty-Three

They clambered over the tiles away from The Willows –
this time via a different, more complicated, route. Beth's
phone rang, forcing her to stop. She answered and started
saying, "Oh no . . . okay . . . I'll be there . . ." She hung
up and turned to Jack. "Mia's sick. Cathy's taking her to
the out-of-hours doctor but wants me to stay with the
others till Pete gets back home. It shouldn't be for very
long. I'll meet you at the hospital as soon as I can."

Once down at street level, they said goodbye. Jack
checked his pocket for his phone, planning on warning
Fabien about Kai, even though he had zero hope that his
friend would answer it – he hadn't answered any of
Jack's previous calls. After a minute's frantic search, the
only thing Jack had found was the little hammer Mrs
Roberts had given him. His heart sank – his phone must
have fallen out of his pocket when his leg went through

the roof. He hurried to the hospital, praying that he wasn't too late.

By the time he entered the building it was after seven o'clock. One of the nurses in the ICU told him Fabien had been transferred from there to a normal ward the previous day. "The luck of the young," she said. "No permanent damage. But he's got severe bruising and took quite a bump on the head, so needs lots of rest." Jack quickly located the ward and found Fabien awake and propped up against a mound of pillows. He looked a thousand times better than the last time Jack had seen him. A plate of congealed pasta lay on the tray table in front of him.

"That looks tasty," said Jack, grinning at the sight of his friend awake.

"My favourite." Fabien gave Jack a wry smile. "I was hoping for sausages."

Jack laughed. "Seriously, I'm glad you're okay. I was worried. How're you feeling?"

"Sore, but not bad," said Fabien.

"What happened on the roof?"

"The last thing I remember is tripping on something. Then I slipped," Fabien confessed. "The rest is a blank, apart from being in the ambulance."

"Did Kai push you?" asked Jack.

Fabien shook his head, then immediately grimaced with pain. "Kai was there, but I slipped."

"That's good."

"What do you mean? Why's it good?" squeaked Fabien.

"Um . . ." *How can I explain the fact that Kai didn't push Fabien off the roof means he probably isn't a homicidal maniac?* Jack took a deep breath and told Fabien what he knew. "We think that Kai wants to stop you blabbing to the police. You need to be on your guard . . . just in case."

Fabien's cheeks turned the colour of paper. "Kai's coming here?"

Jack cast a nervous glance at the other occupied beds in the ward. "Kai won't try anything when there are witnesses."

Fabien exhaled. "But what about Grandad? Kai might hurt him."

"Kai just wants to protect himself and his uncle. Your grandad doesn't know anything, so he's no danger to them." *Unlike you*, Jack nearly added.

"Grandad's got a gemstone." Fabien winced as he shifted in the bed. "He won't give it up without a fight."

"That's only a problem if Kai and Bill know about it," said Jack slowly. "They don't know, do they?"

Fabien turned his large saucer eyes on Jack. "Kai knows, but I didn't tell him, I swear. He went on and on,

asking where Grandad kept it. He said I had to find it . . .
I was gonna warn Grandad, but then this happened . . ."

Jack gulped, remembering Mr G flashing his stone
around in the lounge. Things had suddenly got even more
serious. How far would Bill and Kai go to find that
diamond? "Okay, so we need to get your grandad to
safety. I'll look after that," he said, while wondering
exactly how he'd be able to save a one-legged eighty-
year-old. "Beth is on her way here. She'll stay with you."

Fabien heaved himself further up on the pillows.
"Have you got any paper?"

Mystified, Jack took one of the Get Well Soon cards
from the bedside cabinet, and under Fabien's directions
found a pen in the drawer. Fabien started scribbling.
After a few minutes he finished, handed Jack the card
and flopped back on his pillows, looking exhausted.

"It's the safest, quickest way to get to Grandad's room
on the second floor from the attic, and from there to the
exit," Fabien explained as Jack looked at the scrappy
map. "There are security cameras at the main doors, at
the front and back. Kai told me once. I've marked the
other cameras with a C."

The scale of Fabien's map was all wrong, and he'd
run out of space, with the reception squashed into the
bottom corner. Still, it gave Jack some idea of where he
had to go. Large Xs marked the attic window and the

entrance doors. Fabien had written "Grandad" in shaky letters, and the number "21" halfway along one of the labyrinthine second-floor corridors.

It was going to be a major challenge to find Mr Garibaldi and get him out without being seen, not to mention what Jack would do with Mr G once he'd rescued him. Take him to Auntie Lil?

While Jack was stuffing the map in his pocket, Fabien swung his legs out of bed. "What are you doing?" said Jack, horrified.

"I'm coming with you."

Jack shook his head. "You're not well enough."

"It should be me going there, not you," said Fabien in a quivery voice, his eyes brimming with tears. "It's my fault we're in this mess."

"Don't be a numbskull. You're not coming with me. Anyway, I'm going to wait with you till Beth arrives," said Jack, wishing she would hurry up.

"No, don't wait! Go now!" Fabien grabbed Jack's sleeve. His grip was surprisingly strong. "Please. Save Grandad. And don't end up dead.'

*

Jack left. What if Beth got held up and couldn't make it to the hospital? What if Kai turned up there? Should Jack have stayed with Fabien? *But* Fabien had begged Jack to go. All the way to The Willows, Fabien's words kept spinning round Jack's head: *Save Grandad, save Grandad, save Grandad.* Jack couldn't bear the thought of anything happening to Mr G. He had to make sure the old man was safe. And Jack prayed that Beth arrived to keep Fabien safe too.

Jack went across the rooftops again, avoiding the route with the broken skylight. Adrenaline and worry pushed him on. He fixed his concentration on where to put his feet in the darkness – one mistake could be fatal. By the time Jack got to the retirement home he was dirty and weary, but he didn't have a moment to rest.

Once inside the building, Jack was quick to make his way down the staircase from the attic. The wing he needed was on the other side of the building. He zipped along, dodging into alcoves when he thought someone was coming, diving left and right around corners. He took a hasty glance at Fabien's map and five minutes later he was outside apartment twenty-one. After checking that all was clear, he knocked. Nothing. He tried the handle. To his amazement, it opened.

"Hello? Mr Garibaldi?" Jack called. He felt bad for trespassing in Mr Garibaldi's apartment. Say he'd gone to bed? The light was on in the hall, giving Jack a view of the sitting room straight in front of him. As he gently closed the front door behind him, he called out again. Again, no response.

The sitting room had a high ceiling and canary-yellow walls. A row of chairs stood under the window at the far end, along with a small dark-wood dining table. A sofa lay to the left facing an enormous TV screen which was on, but with the sound muted. There was the whiff of furniture polish, like the stuff Auntie Lil used in her house. The only sound was the ticking of a large wall clock.

Two bedrooms and a kitchen also led off the hallway. All empty. Jack quickly checked the bathroom and moments later was back outside the apartment and creeping along the corridor. Where was Mr G? Having dinner in the restaurant? In the lounge? Visiting a friend? Kidnapped? Or worse? Jack swallowed that thought, but the longer he spent searching for Mr G, the more likely *he'd* be caught.

As Jack deliberated what to do, a distinctive voice filtered to him from further along the corridor. He tiptoed that way, peeked around the corner and saw Mr Garibaldi chatting to Jolly. Mr G was all right! Jack hesitated – neither Mr Garibaldi nor the security guard looked in any hurry to finish their conversation. Jack ducked back around the corner, thinking hard. He couldn't very well interrupt them and say to Mr Garibaldi, "Hi, your life's in danger. You need to leave straight away," could he? Fabien's grandad would wonder what was going on. And as Nina had banned Jack from the home, Jolly would simply throw him out, no questions asked. No, Jack had to think of another way to get Mr G to safety.

A slight sound came from behind him. Before Jack had time to turn, a gloved hand was clamped against his mouth, stifling his scream.

Chapter Twenty-Four

"Shhh," said Beth in Jack's ear, and slowly released her grip.

"What are you doing?" said Jack in an angry whisper, rubbing his lips, chafed by her woollen gloves. Jack glanced down the corridor and pulled her into Mr G's apartment, through to the sitting room.

"Thank goodness I've found you . . ." Beth was puffing, her normally pale face raspberry red. "I was about to give up—"

"Did anyone see you?" he cut in, half-annoyed at her for the fright she'd given him, half-relieved to see her.

"No . . . I was careful. It's taken ages to find you though." She sounded a bit choked up. "Didn't you get my messages?"

He shook his head. "I've lost my phone. What's happened?"

"Fabien's disappeared from the hospital. They've called the police."

Jack's heart did an unpleasant flip. "He's probably hiding from Kai, or maybe he's gone home?"

"You reckon?" Beth arched a sweaty eyebrow. "Because that *wouldn't* be the first place the hospital would check. You don't think he's . . . ?" She drew a line across her neck.

"Course not," snapped Jack, but guilt gnawed at him – he'd left Fabien alone and defenceless in the hospital. "But Kai knows about Mr Garibaldi's gemstone. Fabien could be on his way here to help his grandad. I told him I'd take care of it, but maybe he just waited until I'd left. We'll wait for Mr G to come back and—"

Jack broke off as he heard the click of the front door opening and hurried footsteps. If it was Mr Garibaldi, he'd suddenly grown another leg. Jack and Beth remained frozen on the spot, staring at each other in horror. Another door creaked open. Jack put his finger to his lips and they tiptoed into the hall. Bumps and thuds came from inside one of the bedrooms. Whoever the intruder was, they were in a real hurry. And there was the faint smell of sickly aftershave again . . .

Before Jack and Beth could hide, Bill appeared in the doorway of a bedroom. "Who are you?" he blustered.

"Who are *you*?" demanded Beth in her haughtiest voice, at the same time edging around him.

"I've got an appointment with Mr Garibaldi. This is private property. You have no right to enter—"

"An appointment in his bedroom?" Beth took another step towards the front door. "You don't want to be mistaken for a thief, do you?"

Bill tightened his fingers into enormous fists. His face had gone crimson. "It's none of your business what I'm doing here."

"Mr Garibaldi is our friend. We're visiting him," said Jack.

"Where is he then?" Bill curled his top lip, and brought out his phone. "I'm calling security. You can explain yourselves to him."

"Okay, call Jolly. We'll ask Mr Garibaldi if he was expecting you, shall we?" Beth went to push past Bill.

The man put out an arm, barring her way. "Not so fast. The front door was open and I came to investigate, that's what I'll say. Who are they going to believe – a pair of kids, or a respected member of the community?"

"You're in our way," said Beth, her dark eyes flashing. "Let me past."

Bill snorted but didn't move. Beth aimed a swift kick at his shin.

"You little . . ." Bill growled, stooping to rub his leg.

Beth grabbed Jack's hand and they fled the apartment, almost knocking Mr G off his feet as they reached the corridor. "You're in an awful rush," Mr Garibaldi said. "Where's the fire?"

"No time to explain," panted Jack. "You're in danger. Come with us."

Fortunately Mr Garibaldi didn't argue, only taking a firm grip of his walking stick and allowing Jack and Beth to shepherd him towards the nearby lift. Luck was on their side because when Beth pressed the button, the lift doors pinged open straight away. They bundled Mr G inside. Jack pressed the button for the ground floor and the doors hissed shut.

Jack wiped his brow. "That man was Bill."

"I guessed that. Hey, you're bleeding again." Beth was eyeing Jack's injured knee with worry.

Jack gave it a dismissive glance and returned his gaze to the lift display panel. His knee throbbed like the bone was being tapped by a woodpecker, but he'd cope. He had to.

Mr G was looking more and more confused with each passing second. "Can one of you explain what the devil is going on?"

"I will, Mr G, but—"

"*Ground floor,*" intoned the automated lift announcement, and the doors swished open.

Jack poked his head out, and looked left along the passage towards the reception, the main doors and . . . freedom. If they could get Mr Garibaldi out of the building, they could return to search for Fabien – before Bill or Kai found him.

They hustled Mr Garibaldi along the corridor towards the reception. Jack spotted a security camera directed at the entrance. Were the main doors unlocked? He really hoped so. He gestured at Beth and Mr G to stop as Jolly came out of the visitors' toilets and sat at the reception desk. The guard turned to the computer screen, put in a pair of earbuds and opened a bag of crisps. Soon Jolly was guffawing and chortling as he settled back in the chair, his feet resting on the desk. If Jack and Beth had been on their own, they could have crept past, no problem. But with Mr Garibaldi with them, creeping wasn't an option.

"Come on." Beth twisted round to go back towards the lounge.

Good plan – maybe we can escape through the patio windows, thought Jack. As he turned away, something in the cubbyhole office snagged Jack's attention. Maybe it was just his imagination playing tricks on him, but it stopped him in his tracks. Suddenly the thing moved and the toe of a trainer stuck out to the left of the door. No, this was real all right. Jack gestured at Beth to stop and wait, and ducked down on all fours with pain screaming through his knee. He crawled along by the wall until he reached the little office.

Fabien was huddled against some shelves, hugging his legs with his arms, his tightly shut eyes squeezing tears down his pallid cheeks. When Jack gently touched his arm, his eyelids sprung open, shock turning to relief as he saw it was Jack. Jack signalled him to follow and they crawled back to the other two.

"Fabien!" said Mr G. "What on earth are you doing here?"

"And *how* did you get here?" said Beth.

"Got a bus, and I sneaked in before Jolly locked the door. I wanted to check you were all right, Grandad." He reached out and gave his grandad a weak hug.

"Of course I'm all right," said Mr G, as they made their way past the lift and on to the lounge. "But I would like to know exactly what is going on, and why you're not in hospital. Have they discharged you?"

Before Fabien could answer, the lounge door opened, Conchita hurried out and rattled towards them with her tea trolley. Jack twisted on his heel, stumbling in his rush, and jammed his finger on the button to summon the lift. Conchita beamed to see them.

"Mr Garibaldi! Hot cocoa in the lounge if you fancy it . . ." She broke off, her smile fading as she recognised Fabien.

"They're visiting me . . . no rule against that," said a smiling Mr G, before Conchita had the chance to say anything. *Quick thinking*, thought Jack in admiration.

"Well, no, but . . ." Conchita's hand fluttered to her throat. "You don't look well, Fabien."

"I'm okay," said Fabien weakly.

Mr Garibaldi put an arm around Fabien's shoulders. "Nothing a good rest won't sort out."

The lift bell pinged and the doors slid open. They stepped into the lift. What should they do? Where should they go? Jack stared at the lift display panel – "B" must be the basement, but he had no idea whether there was an exit that way. The top button showed "2", so Jack pressed that one, willing the doors to shut before Conchita asked more questions. And they *did* start to close. But it was too late. The toe of a polished black shoe appeared in the gap, and the doors bounced open again.

Chapter Twenty-Five

"You again." Bill looked as shocked to see them as they were him, but he recovered quickly and reached forwards to stop the lift closing again. Conchita now stood directly in front of the open lift with her tea trolley, gawping at what must have been a really weird scene of Bill straddling the threshold, while Jack, Beth, Fabien and Mr Garibaldi huddled inside.

"What's going on?" Conchita asked.

"Bill's the thief," said Beth. "Call the police!"

"Wha . . . ?" Conchita's mouth fell open further, if that was possible.

"Don't listen to them," said Bill. "Fetch Jolly, will you, Conchita? I found these two wandering around Mr G's apartment."

"Nonsense," said Mr G. "They're my guests."

"Well, I don't know . . ." Conchita's hand moved to her throat once more. "I think everyone needs to come out and we'll sort everything."

Jack put his hands up as if in surrender and took a slow step out of the lift. Bill instinctively moved sideways to make room for him. Jack grabbed the trolley and shoved it hard towards Bill. It hit him in the stomach and he stumbled backwards, sending piles of mugs and plates crashing to the floor. Conchita let out a scream. Jack jumped into the lift again and Beth slammed her thumb on the button for the second floor. Their last view was of Bill's puce face, as he attempted to extricate himself from trolley wheels and broken china.

Jack looked at the others. Fabien was leaning against the corner of the lift walls, looking green, with Mr Garibaldi half-supporting him. Beth's chin jutted out in grim determination. Jack swiped a hand over his brow, sticky from sweat and the sun cream he'd plastered on that morning. It seemed such a long time ago.

"We can't ride up and down in this lift all night," said Beth.

Think, Jack, think. Every nerve in his body jangled. The others were depending on him to sort everything out. He owed it to Fabien. He took a deep breath. "We'll hide in the attic."

His stomach flipped as the lift lurched to a halt on the second floor. Minutes later they were in the attic corridor. Beth surged ahead, running through a fire door and into an even narrower passageway. Jack had lost his bearings.

"Are you sure this is the right way?" Jack muttered.

"Trust me. I remember that picture." She pointed at a framed wall print of sheep in a field. "I'm right, aren't I, Fabien?" Fabien nodded but looked too sick to say anything.

After passing five or six rooms, Beth stopped and flung open a door. They ushered Mr G and Fabien inside and threw the bolt across, plunging them into semi-darkness until Fabien flicked a switch and a single bulb hanging from the ceiling illuminated the room. They were safe for the moment, although Jack was still feeling jittery.

"Help me." Beth was busy pushing an old desk against the door. Jack joined her, thoughts running helter-skelter through his mind. Things were getting trickier by the second. How were they going to get an eighty-year-old and an injured Fabien out of The Willows? A sharp stab from his knee reminded Jack of his own injury. On inspection, he saw old, dried blood had stained the edges of the rip in his jeans, but every time he bent his leg, he felt the chill of fresh blood.

"You look like hell," said Beth to Fabien, as she helped him and Mr G sit on one of the many packing crates. "You should be in hospital. They're looking for you."

"But I couldn't lie around thinking Grandad was in danger . . ." Fabien trailed off, as if running out of energy to talk.

"What danger? And what's this about Bill being a thief?" said Mr G. He gazed at each of them in turn, his watery grey eyes blinking rapidly behind his glasses. Strands of hair had escaped its band, and snowy wisps drifted out from the sides of his head. "I wish someone would explain what on earth is going on. Why are we hiding?"

No one spoke. Then Fabien gave a shaky sigh. "Bill and Kai have been stealing from people. And now they're looking for your diamond, Grandad."

"Oh, never mind about the stone. It's safe where it is," said Mr G, with a dismissive wave of his hand. "So it's been Bill all along. I never did trust him. But who's Kai?"

"Bill's nephew," said Beth.

"What did you mean by 'all along'?" said Jack, ignoring her and staring at Mr G.

Fabien's grandad blew out. "Uff, it's a long story. No time to go into all that now. If they're after us, we'd better scarper."

187

Scarpering was the last thing Mr G could do, thought Jack as he hitched himself onto the corner of the old desk to rest. Every inch of his body ached, and his injured knee throbbed. The worry about Fabien, Nina accusing Jack of the thefts, the police wanting to interview him, and now trying to rescue Mr Garibaldi and Fabien . . . it had all taken its toll on Jack. And on Beth, too. She turned her hollow, tired eyes towards him and gave a small smile.

"Where's your phone?" he asked.

"I left it at home by mistake, and I didn't have time to go back for it. I've got this though." She brought out a head torch and handed it to Jack. "It's from the camping trip. I thought it might be useful."

Jack nodded. "Good thinking, but right now we need to call the police." He turned to Fabien. "Have you got your phone?'

Fabien shook his head. "My mum must have taken it from the hospital."

"Mr G?"

"I'm afraid I don't own one," said Mr Garibaldi.

Fear stabbed Jack behind the ribs. He cursed under his breath – they were running out of options. Beth went to the window and looked out through the smeared, dirty pane. "There's one way we could go. Back over the rooftops."

Jack opened his mouth to argue, then shut it again. It was a ridiculous idea . . . and yet did they have any choice? It was that way or no way.

Fabien summoned up enough strength to say, "We can't! What about Grandad?"

"What *about* me?" said Mr G.

"You can't go on the roofs," said Fabien, looking even sicker at the thought.

"Nonsense, I'm as fit as a fiddle. Nothing wrong with me. Had my check-up with the doc last week. I might have a dodgy leg, but I've got the stamina of a lion." As if to prove the point, Mr G hobbled over to the window, hoisted himself, with only a little struggle, onto the table next to Beth, and stuck his head out of the small skylight. "It's a fine night."

It struck Jack that Mr G wasn't the biggest problem. The problem was Fabien. He should have been in hospital. Plus, Jack knew the roofs frightened Fabien. And he had to admit it, he was frightened too. Scrap that, he was terrified.

The attic doorknob rattled, making everyone jump.

Malcolm's voice came from the other side. "Jack, Beth, Mr Garibaldi? Are you in there?"

"Don't say anything," whispered Jack. "He'll go away."

But he didn't. Instead, Malcolm clearly said to someone, "They must be in here. It only locks from the inside." Then, louder, he added, "Mr Garibaldi, we're worried about you and Fabien."

"Open the door, and we'll sort out this misunderstanding." That was Bill.

"Nobody's in trouble," said Malcolm. "Everything can be sorted in a jiffy."

Jack gestured at the others to keep quiet. Could they trust Malcolm? For all they knew, Bill had told the manager that they were the thieves. Worse still, maybe Malcolm was a thief too? It wasn't a risk Jack was prepared to take. Outside, there was frantic muttering, then everything went quiet. Jack let out a breath – had Malcolm given up?

Thwack! Thwack! The flimsy wood suddenly juddered as if someone was throwing their weight against it. Each wallop shuddered through the panels like a mini earthquake, shaking not only the door but the desk and the floorboards beneath their feet. Bill and Malcolm weren't going to give up – they weren't going to go away until they got into the room.

Jack put on Beth's head torch. The tight elasticated strap rubbed against the itchy, sensitive skin of his brow. Then he helped Fabien across to the window. He noticed a length of rope on one of the packing crates – *Could be useful*, he thought – and looped it over his shoulder, across his body. It didn't weigh much and fitted snugly around him. Beth hooked the window as wide as it would go, and fresh, cool air gusted in. With a combination of pushing and pulling, they manhandled first Mr Garibaldi, then Fabien through the narrow gap. When the others were safe, Jack hoisted himself up and through the window. The fresh breeze and freedom made Jack instantly calmer. But it didn't last long. Beneath the caws of the gulls above and the faint rush of traffic far below, the rhythmic slamming against the attic door continued.

Jack was searching around in the vain hope of finding something to bar the window with when a violent crack rang out. There was no time left.

Jack's last view through the dirty pane was of the door panel splintering and a hand appearing to wrestle with the lock. He turned his back, took Fabien's arm and made off across the roof.

Chapter Twenty-Six

Mr Garibaldi was fitter than Jack had realised. In contrast, Fabien looked like a corpse. Beth was doing her best to chivvy him along, but with every tug he groaned out loud. The first incline was easy enough – a gentle slope, with grippy, rough tiles and a brick wall divide to one side that they used to help steady themselves. Mr Garibaldi shuffled down the other side on his bum.

The night sky burnt orange from the hundreds of city street lamps. The moon, a pale disc, disappeared and reappeared between drifting clouds. There was enough light to see the outlines of the roofs and the silhouettes of the others, but not much more. Jack was glad of the head torch for extra light, but it flickered as if the battery was about to die.

With the collapsed skylight blocking one escape route, they had no choice but to go the more complicated route he and Beth had used. In his head, Jack counted how many more roofs they'd have to cross before reaching the safety of ground level. The answer was a scary fifteen. It seemed like an impossible challenge.

They ploughed on. It was tough, exhausting work. Each rooftop was different – some had loads of trip hazards, others were more straightforward. Some of the steep slopes took a tortuous ten or fifteen minutes to scale, clambering up slippery grey slates with no handholds, and just as long to descend the other side.

They arrived at the steepest of them all. Jack and Beth had negotiated the roof before with no problem. But that was then. They huddled at the bottom, gazing up at a sheer face of glistening slate. Jack took a deep breath and exchanged a panicked glance with Beth. How on earth were they going to get Mr G and Fabien to the top of *that*? It wasn't far, but it was steep. So steep. And dark. One wrong move could mean a broken limb . . . or worse.

"Well," said Mr Garibaldi cheerily. "We'd better get a move on."

Nothing seemed to faze him, but Fabien looked as if he was about to throw up. Jack took Beth's elbow and pulled her aside, a plan half-forming in his mind. "We're going to need to tie ourselves together with this." He pulled the rope he'd discovered in the attic from his shoulder.

Beth gazed at it and then at his face, uncertainly. "Are you mad? If one of us trips, we'll all fall."

He shook his head. "If Mr G or Fabien slips, we will stop them sliding right to the bottom. I hope."

"But you're not sure."

"Not a hundred per cent, no."

Beth was silent, as if mulling it over. "Okay, let's go for it," she said, with grit in her voice.

With her help, Jack tied the rope around the others' waists like a mountaineer's safety cord, linking them close together, then tied the end over his shoulder and back around his waist. They started up the incline. Jack kept Fabien close to him, so they were moving in tandem. Step by tiny step, crouched low, Jack searched for the tiniest crevice to cling on to, then placed Fabien's fingertips or foot in the right position, before moving on.

Every few centimetres he crawled, Jack called commands down to Beth, like, "Fingerhold at ten o'clock, toehold at five, broken tile at twelve." He didn't know if it helped her, but he felt better saying it – more in control. After what felt like an eternity, the ridge was within their reach.

"A few more steps," he urged Fabien.

Suddenly, the rope gave a violent jerk, wrenching Jack and Fabien backwards. Fabien let out a cry of pain. The rope chafed the skin of Jack's shoulder and neck, as he turned to see what had happened. In the faint torchlight he picked out the shapes of Beth and Mr G. Fabien's grandad had slipped and lay face down on the tiles.

"It's okay, I've got him," shouted Beth. And she *did* have him. She grasped him by the upper arm and helped him find his balance again. Jack exhaled, the blood roaring in his ears. His plan had worked – the rope had held.

They moved on, but everyone was tiring. When Jack thought they were far enough away from The Willows, Jack and Beth untied the rope and they all sat for a rest on the tiles in a shallow valley between two peaks. It was sheltered from the worst of the biting wind, and even better, no windows or terraces overlooked the area. All the same, Jack kept an eye open for signs of trouble. Threatening clouds were building up and now all but covered the moon. Jack felt the first fine droplet of rain land on his cheek.

"Do you think they're looking for us?" Beth cast an anxious glance over her shoulder.

"Bill and Malcolm won't come up here," Jack replied. "Kai's the one we've got to worry about. Where is he?"

"Maybe he'll leave us alone and make a run for it," said Fabien.

Jack's pulse quickened as he caught a glimpse of Fabien's sweaty cheeks in the light of his torch. The boy looked so ill. "We won't be safe until we've put a proper distance between us and them. Then we can get to the ground and call the police."

"I don't have a phone, but I've got this." Mr G rummaged in his jacket pocket and brought out a crumpled bar of chocolate. "Emergency rations. Always come prepared." He broke off four pieces and handed them around. "For energy."

Jack took it gratefully, but Fabien handed his piece back to his grandad with a weak shake of the head. Jack's belly gave a loud growl, reminding him that he'd had nothing to eat since lunchtime. The chocolate was welcome but cloyed up his mouth – he longed for some water to wash it down.

He went back up to the ridge to keep a lookout. A deep exhaustion had wedged itself in his bones. Were they mad bringing Fabien and Mr Garibaldi onto the roofs? Say things went wrong? The responsibility made Jack's fragile skin sting, and his bashed knee throbbed under Beth's makeshift scarf bandage.

He turned his attention to what lay ahead. The route was perilous, that was a fact. And there was no avoiding it – unless they took an even longer way around, meaning extra kilometres on treacherous roofs. And that would put them at more risk of being caught. Mr Garibaldi was doing fine. Fabien, on the other hand, was getting weaker by the minute. And Jack had noticed the fear in his eyes. This wasn't the place to have an attack of nerves. Strength was needed. Bucketloads. Jack wasn't convinced that Fabien had enough. He'd witnessed him wobble and nearly fall. He'd seen him shake so much he'd been almost unable to stand.

"Will you stop pacing?" said Beth, coming up behind Jack. "It's not helping."

"It helps me. Anyway, somebody's got to keep watch." His nerves were frazzled. Sitting for too long made him uneasy. They were vulnerable up there. Plus, proper drizzle had started. Jack shook a damp strand of sun-cream-coated hair from his eyes as he squinted again at the route they'd have to take. There was no going back. He returned to Fabien and Mr Garibaldi. "What were you saying back in the attic about the thieves?"

Mr G stretched out his real leg and flexed the foot. "Well, I have a small confession to make. I hired a private detective."

"You did what?" said Fabien, sitting up straighter.

"Someone had to do something. Malcolm's worried a scandal will affect business, but I knew there was something fishy going on. So I decided to take matters into my own hands."

"Wait a sec," said Beth from by Jack's side. "Who is this detective?"

"A friend of mine, working undercover," said Mr Garibaldi calmly, as if it were the most normal thing in the world to get a mate to infiltrate a retirement home and spy on people. "We were trying to lure the criminals into the open. The more pressure they felt under, the more likely they'd be to make mistakes."

"Your blue diamond was bait?" said Jack slowly.

Mr Garibaldi gave a chuckle. "Something like that."

"Why didn't you tell me?" said Fabien, resting his head on his grandad's shoulder.

Mr G put his arm around his grandson and gave a squeeze. "I didn't want you to be dragged into it all. I suppose that didn't work though. I had no idea about this Kai chap being involved. No idea at all. When all this is over, you'll have to explain your part in all this."

The cogs of Jack's brain ground slowly as he grappled with what Mr G had said. A friend of Mr G. Could it be—? Jack's thoughts were cut off by an ugly yell. He spun round, his guts twisting. Kai stood on a ridge, five roofs behind them, his form silhouetted against the glowing city skyline.

Chapter Twenty-Seven

"Let's go!" Jack shouted to the others, as Kai lumbered down the slope and disappeared from view. Jack willed his stressed brain to work, but it was as if it had gone on strike. *Think, Jack, think.* How long would it take Kai to reach them? He was fit and strong, but not an expert jumper. And he was clumsy. Two or three minutes per roof. Five roofs. That would be ten to fifteen brief minutes.

The others heaved themselves to their feet once more, Beth and Mr Garibaldi each grasping one of Fabien's elbows. Jack ducked under a big ventilation pipe and then crouched and slithered onto a flatter roof. Goosebumps sprung up on his forearms from the fierce breeze as he scoured the area, angling his torch beam. He'd landed in what resembled a hidden rooftop courtyard. The blank side of an office block lay straight ahead, rising ten metres in the air. No footholds, no handholds, only bare concrete and brick. To his left, another high wall rose at right angles to the first. No way around there either. A parapet was to his right. He made his way over and peered down at the sheer drop to the street. He saw headlights and heard the distant rumble of cars, made noisier by wet tarmac. Shady silhouettes of people hurried to and fro under the street lamps, oblivious to what was going on way above them. The parapet ended at the corner of the office block, the front face of which looked onto the drop to the street. It had six large windows with roughly thirty-centimetre-deep ledges, at the same level as the parapet. Safety lay on the roof to the other side of that building.

Jack turned away, trying to control the surge of panic rising in his chest. How was he going to get them all to safety? The odds were stacked against them. Beth arrived with the others. She left Fabien slumped against a wall, his head bowed between his knees, and came over.

"You're thinking of going that way?" She pointed at the line of windows.

"Yeah. We take one each – you with Mr G and me with Fabien," said Jack, attempting to sound confident.

Beth fiddled with the chain around her neck, the metal glinting in the torchlight. Jack saw that the anatomical heart locket from her mum and dad had taken the place of the little key. "Can't we fight it out with Kai?" she said. "There are four of us, and only one of him."

Jack shoved his hands in his pockets in an attempt to warm his frozen fingers. "Look at us – I've got a bashed knee, Fabien is so weak he can barely stand, and then there's Mr G. What are our chances against Kai?"

"What about if you go alone to get help? I'll distract Kai."

"No way! You can't do that *and* keep Mr G and Fabien safe."

"All right. Take Fabien, and leave Mr G with me." Beth leant against the parapet, facing him. He couldn't make out her expression. "Face facts, Jack – you might not be able to save everybody."

"So you're saying I should save myself and Fabien, and to hell with you and Mr G? We're in this together. We stay together." A nerve twitched under his right eye. Rubbing it, he said, "Do you trust me?"

"Course I do. We're mates." She said it without hesitation.

Joy surged through him on hearing those words, despite the sick feeling swirling in his stomach. "Then trust me now."

Jack gazed at Fabien and Mr Garibaldi as they hobbled over to him. Then he thought of Bill and Kai –

criminals hell-bent on success – and pulled his shoulders back. "We can't go back, and there's no time to find another route. We have to go forwards. There's no choice." It was hardly the pep talk he'd hoped would spring from his lips at a moment like that. "There's a way to get around this building, but we have to climb along there." He pointed to the wall of windows. "The ledges are wide enough for us to step on. It won't be easy, but we can all do it."

"I can't," said Fabien, his enormous eyes widening in horror. "Go on without me. I'll only slow you down."

"You can do this. There are places to hold on to. We'll help you." Jack gripped Fabien's arms, looking him straight in the eyes. "Trust me." It was the second time he'd said that in as many minutes.

Mr G placed his hand on Fabien's shoulder. "Come on, my boy. Time to go."

"What about you?" sobbed Fabien.

"I'm as tough as army boots," said the old man. "Don't worry about me."

The six windows along the stretch of wall that lay between them and safety were spaced a metre apart, the first window a short half-metre hop along from the end of the parapet. A cool yellow light shone from the windows, illuminating the wide concrete ledge below each pane. A weak hope fluttered through Jack's mind that someone working really late in the offices would see them and let them into the building. Then he remembered it was Sunday – nobody would be there right now.

"Hold on to me, Mr Garibaldi," said Beth. "Do what I do."

Jack and Beth pulled Mr G onto the parapet, as tiny fragments of stone crumbled away in a grainy shower. Once steady, he stood upright, showing no fear, but Jack was all too aware of the chasm beneath them. Beth went first and handled the step onto the ledge like a pro. She faced the window, hanging on to a lip above the pane of glass with her right hand. Now for Mr Garibaldi.

"Give me the end of your walking stick, Mr G." He held out his stick to Beth, keeping a firm hold of the handle, his other hand gripping the corner of the wall. Jack put a hand on his back to support him and watched, his stomach churning like a washing machine. With snail-like speed, the old man reached one foot onto the ledge, then the other. Jack watched, heart in mouth, as he wobbled, his false leg wavering in the air. Mr G's shoe flew off, disappearing into the nothingness.

Beth pulled on the stick, and Mr G planted his leg on the ledge. She grasped him around his shoulders. "I've got you."

Jack let out a hiss of relief as Mr Garibaldi steadied himself, his face a picture of concentration. There was no time for Jack and Fabien to wait until Beth and Mr G had reached the safety of the other side of the office block – one glance behind showed him that Kai was at the top of a neighbouring ridge. Two minutes, three tops, and he'd be on their roof.

"Don't look down," said Jack to Fabien. "Keep looking at me."

Jack felt Fabien's bony juddering heaviness as he helped him onto the parapet. He seemed too weak to take any of his own weight. The drizzle had become more persistent and fat droplets bounced off the stonework.

"We have to move faster, mate," said Jack urgently.

"I can't."

We'll die if we stay here, Jack wanted to say, but stopped himself. His heart was pounding, though. Soon Kai would be on them. He'd be able to push them into oblivion. "If your grandad can do it, so can you."

Fabien looked up at him, terror in his eyes, but started shuffling along the stone. Jack coaxed him towards the first window. Fabien stumbled as he took the step onto the ledge, but miraculously secured his footing. Jack removed Fabien's quaking hand from where it gripped his hoodie and curled the boy's fingers around the lip above the window. "You're doing great," he said. "Hold on tight."

Jack got ready to hop onto the window ledge next to Fabien.

CRACK!

A large piece of stone fell from the parapet, taking Jack's foothold with it. He stumbled, off balance, his arms spiralling in the air. His heart rose in his throat as he dropped. Instinctively, Jack reached out to grip the remaining stone with shaky hands, digging his wet fingers into the slippery, damp concrete while his legs scissored in the air. Fabien shrieked. Jack's stomach lurched as the lit street tipped and tilted below him. He attempted to swing his legs towards the wall face beneath, grappling for a toehold in the brick, as pain seared through his injured knee. But the parapet formed a deep overhang and Jack was only met with space.

Through the fuzzy ache of strained muscles, he heard Beth shout something, but the breeze snatched the words away. A clatter came from somewhere above him. As Jack's fingers grappled for a better grip, he touched something hard and cold. Mrs Roberts's hammer! It must have fallen from his pocket when he'd slipped. He curled his fingers around it as the dark shape of Kai loomed above him, his face a sickly yellow in the light from Jack's head torch.

"Where's Fabien?" Kai thumped his large foot on the concrete. With his forearm resting on his knee, he craned over the parapet. Jack smelt cigarette smoke on Kai's breath, mixed with sour sweat. Dread pulsed through him. If Kai turned, he'd spot Fabien still clinging to the first window. He locked eyes with Kai, holding his stare, not even daring to blink. Kai leant further over the parapet, as if expecting to see Fabien clinging to Jack's legs. Then his gaze shifted to where Jack's tired, frozen fingers clamped themselves vice-like to the rough concrete. Jack tried to slow his breaths, forcing them in and out between his teeth. He had to think fast. "Bill's got you doing his dirty work for him." Jack's words squeaked out.

Kai snorted. "Not true. Answer the question, dimwit, where's Fabien?"

"What kind of uncle would do that?" Jack ploughed on, his voice stronger now. He was desperately playing for time, hoping against hope that Fabien would overcome his nerves and get moving. "You want to be his dogsbody all your life? Always having to do what he tells you?"

"Hey, I'm in charge up here. He trusts me."

"He trusts you to follow his orders. Where is he when things get tough?" Jack shifted to gain a better grip of the parapet, manoeuvring the hammer into position. "Where is he now? He treats you like dirt."

Another snort from Kai. "Soon I'll be my own man, when I get my share. Then I'll be leaving this dump of a city."

"You think he's gonna give you your share? Nah, I don't think so. You'll end up in prison, but Bill will get away with everything. That's his plan. He's probably escaping right now."

"Shut it, you know nothing 'bout it," said Kai, but Jack heard a flicker of doubt in his voice.

For how long could Fabien cling on? For how long could *Jack* cling on? He blinked up at Kai, nausea clawing at his throat. Kai seemed to be wavering. Maybe some of his words had hit home. But time was running out . . . Jack swallowed hard – his strength was fast disappearing.

Suddenly, Kai leant over the edge and gripped Jack's left arm. "Tell me where that boy is, and I'll help you up."

Now! With his last dribble of strength, Jack plunged the claw head of the hammer into Kai's hand as hard as he dared. Kai shrieked, loosening his grip on Jack's arm, and staggered back, the tiny hammer still embedded in his flesh. Jack willed himself to move, but every sinew in his body ached and stung . . . stretched to its limit. His shoulders to his fingertips screamed in agony. Even his bones throbbed. *Get a grip, Jack.* He almost giggled at the joke. He shook his head to clear the black dots fogging the edges of his vision. Something wet trickled down his cheek. *A tear? Am I crying?*

In a distant part of his consciousness, Jack heard shouts, and a bellow. Then silence.

Was this how his life was going to finish? His crushed and bloodied body would be found on the pavement below, surrounded by a crowd of horrified onlookers? What would happen to Beth? To Fabien and Mr Garibaldi? What about Mum? Dad? Auntie Lil? Jack squeezed his eyelids shut. It really was true. Your life *did* flash in front of you when faced with death. How soon would the end come? How would it feel? In the far reaches of his brain, he heard someone calling his name.

"Jack!" There it was again. The voice came from above him.

His eyes snapped open, half-expecting Kai's leering face to greet him. Instead, Beth was leaning over the edge of the parapet. Fabien was beside her. They had hold of both of his arms. Their hands radiated warmth through his sleeves to his skin. *She came back for me! They came back.*

"I've got you," Beth said. "Let go."

That was madness. *If I let go, I'll fall*, he wanted to say, but the words refused to leave his mouth. He didn't want to die – he had too much living to do.

"Trust me, Jack."

Blood roared in his ears. Random thoughts spiralled through his mind. Beth, Fabien, Mr G . . . trust . . . His only chance. His life depended on them, on Beth. He squeezed his eyelids shut and let go.

Chapter Twenty-Eight

"Is he dead?"

Voices came from far away. Jack prised his eyes open, and Fabien's and Beth's faces swam into view. "Pretty sure I'm still alive," he croaked. Battered and sore, but alive.

"Man, you really freaked me out." Jack squinted sideways. Fabien was slumped next to him, looking worried and pale.

Jack moved his gaze back to the rooftop courtyard where he lay on his back, in a puddle of the recent rain which thankfully had slowed to a light trickle again. The moon reappeared from behind the dark clouds, casting a weak glow on the surface of the roof. Jack gingerly prodded his arms and legs – all there – and struggled to sit up, hissing through his teeth as a spasm of pain rocketed along his fingers. The middle finger of his left hand bulged to one side, the bruising already visible around the joint. He hadn't even been aware he'd injured it.

"I had to bring Fabien back," said Beth. "To reach you quickly. By the way, the hammer move was cool. The way you rammed it into Kai's hand like that."

Jack shuddered at the memory of the metal claw striking flesh and sinew. "It made me want to chuck, though. Where is Kai?"

"He legged it. I think he knows it's game over," she said, grinning.

"And Mr G?"

"Don't worry. He's made it on to the next roof."

"You saved my life . . ." said Jack.

Beth nudged him with the toe of her black boot. "I'd never have left you."

Despite the chilly air, he felt his cheeks redden and an itchy heat spread across his scalp.

"Anyway, how would I get these two down without your help?" she continued. "Come on, let's get going."

That sounded more like the Beth he knew. He rocked to his feet, then shut his eyes for a few seconds, waiting for a giddy wave to pass.

Beth's gasp made Jack open them quickly again. She was fumbling at her neck. "My chain! It's gone."

They hunted around, but in the dark it was impossible to find something so small.

"It's lost," she said. "Doesn't matter." But Jack knew that it did. He got on his hands and knees to scour the area. "It's got to be here somewhere . . ."

"Leave it," said Beth. "We've got to go."

Defeated, Jack nodded and allowed her to pull him back to his feet. He took hold of one of Fabien's arms, Beth the other, and they propelled him once more onto the parapet and towards the first window ledge. Fabien seemed to find a hidden strength. Maybe seeing what had happened to Jack had made him think he'd better just do it. Sandwiched between Jack and Beth, he hopped from one ledge to another without even a squeal. But Jack was fighting wave after wave of nausea. His fingers, his knee, his entire body throbbed. Pure adrenaline made him place one foot in front of the other until, finally, they dropped onto the relative safety of the next roof, to a waiting Mr Garibaldi.

"Got to keep moving," Jack said to the others, once they'd caught their breath and Mr G had hugged all of them. Jack didn't believe that Kai would give up. Thankfully, after a few short steps and one final red-tiled pitch, the welcome dark outline of the tall vent pipe and zip wire appeared silhouetted against the moonlit sky. It was just as he and Beth had left it, what seemed a lifetime ago. They had made it. Jack felt like cheering.

"Remarkable," said Mr Garibaldi, surveying the line. "Reminds me of my childhood. We had one like this slung from the trees in our garden."

Jack took the thin rope he was still carrying and knotted it onto the handle clip, keeping hold of the very end of the rope. Beth went first, carrying Mr G's walking stick and making light work of the brief trip across the gap. Jack dragged the zip-wire handle back with the rope. His fingers trembled as he used his own belt to secure Mr G around his chest and under his armpits to the handle. His trousers rode up, revealing his shins – one pink, one black and shiny. Jack gulped hard. Was it madness to send the old man swinging across the gap?

"Hold tight," Jack said. Mr G hung lopsided like a saggy bag of potatoes with legs.

"Is it a long way down?" Fabien's grandad peered into the dark abyss.

"No, not far." The alleyway was a good thirty metres below them, but Jack thought it best not to mention that. As Mr G swung away from the rooftop, his long hair came loose, billowing behind like a silver-grey streamer.

Relief flooded Jack when, seconds later, he felt Beth's tug on the rope, and he pulled the handle with his belt still attached back again.

"You're next," Jack said to a shaky Fabien, as he steered him towards the zip wire.

It took precious seconds to tie the weak, tired boy to the handle. Jack did his best to cheer him on, telling him they were almost safe, that once on the other side there was no way Kai could reach them. When he had finally satisfied himself that Fabien was secured safely, Jack gave him a shove off the roof.

The next second, a thud came from behind. The dark, lumbering form of Kai panted up the incline towards Jack. In a rush, he whipped his hoodie off and threw it over the zip wire, like an improvised harness. He kicked off from the roof as Kai lunged at his legs. With an angry roar, Jack lashed out with his good leg, hitting the older boy in the thigh. It was enough to make Kai lose his grip. A moment later Jack was in the air, whizzing along the zip wire.

Faster and faster. Halfway there.

Then slower.

And slower.

And he stopped.

Something was wrong. Jack wasn't moving. Now he was suspended above the alleyway. He tried to propel himself forwards by lurching his body from side to side, backwards and forwards, any way he could. Nothing worked. Alarm fizzed through his veins. He aimed his head torch upwards. The wire sagged alarmingly. There wasn't enough momentum to reach the lower roof. He was stuck.

The wire vibrated, and with a jolt sagged further. Jack squinted back towards Kai. Only he wasn't on the roof. Instead, a dark figure had joined him on the wire.

"Go back!" he yelled. "It's gonna break!" Jack saw Kai stop, as if considering what to do. Jack didn't wait to see if he turned back. He wound his arms around the zip wire and another hot spasm shot down his injured finger. Jack bit the insides of his cheeks hard and tasted hot, salty blood. Groaning aloud, he swung his legs up so that his heels were curled around the wire. He now hung like a sloth. His hoodie dropped and was swallowed by the evening gloom.

"Come on," Jack muttered to himself, shaking hair, slick with sweat, from his face. He shuffled along – towards Beth and the others, away from Kai – right hand, left leg, then the opposites. He contracted his stomach muscles. It made him feel lighter, more in control. Right, left, left, right . . .

Breathe, he told himself . . . in . . . out . . . in . . . out. Each movement along the wire reverberated through his hurt leg and from his fingers, up his arms, into his neck. Exhaustion filled every pore of his skin, every muscle fibre, but he couldn't stop moving. If he did, he wasn't sure he'd be able to get going again.

A few metres to go. Jack calculated that he was over a flat roof about ten metres below him, even though it wasn't visible in the dimness. The wire was sagging more and more. One last push was all he needed. Jack risked taking a peek at Kai. It seemed as if he'd had the sense to turn back.

A creak, a lurch. The contents of Jack's belly shot up to his throat as he was catapulted downwards, still clinging onto the zip wire. He braced himself for the pain that was to come. His arms, elbows, legs scraped against concrete and brick as he crashed into the wall in front of him.

"Aargh!" Jack let go of the wire and dropped like a stone. He landed more or less on his feet, but his legs buckled under him and he collapsed, the back of his skull smacking the gravelled roof.

He must have blacked out because when he opened his eyes, Beth was there, telling him not to move . . . laughing and crying at the same time . . . saying she was glad he'd died, or that he hadn't died . . . something like that . . . And Mr Garibaldi was there too. And Fabien looking shaky, but still on his feet. Jack's body ached, and he thought he might throw up. Then he was on a stretcher or something and being hoisted off the flat roof somehow. Then in an ambulance, its sirens blaring.

And Jack closed his eyes.

Chapter Twenty-Nine

It was the following afternoon. Jack had been discharged from hospital late that morning and they were back in his flat, sipping hot tea with a relieved-looking Auntie Lil. She had insisted that Mr G sleep over until the police had stopped crawling all over The Willows. Mr G had been happy with the idea, as he'd said Fabien's mum and dad "had enough to worry about with Fabien". Mum was on her way back home. Jack hadn't managed to calm her down when he'd called her. She'd said that they needed "a serious chat". Jack wasn't looking forward to that conversation. Dad had looked shocked when Jack had video-called him, but only said, "You all right, son?" and that he'd ask for time off the next week to visit. *Great!* thought Jack.

As he sipped his tea, Jack thought back to the events of the last few days. He'd ended up with five stitches in his knee, two sprained fingers, a shedload of grazes and a bump on the back of his head. His skin had taken a battering, and the doctors had given him a course of strong antibiotics, telling Jack to take care of it over the coming days – something he knew he'd have to do from experience.

Mr Garibaldi had spoken to the police at the hospital and explained his part in it all, while Jack, Beth and Fabien were being checked over by the doctors. Then the officers had interviewed Jack and Beth. A whirr of radio activity had followed as they organised a search of The Willows.

"We'll have a word with you tomorrow," one of the police officers had told a weak but okay Fabien, as a porter wheeled him off to the ward to keep him under observation. After all, he shouldn't have left the hospital in the first place.

An hour later, one of the officers had come back to the cubicle where Jack and Beth had been waiting.

"I've got good news." She'd smiled at them both. "Thanks to you lot, Bill Slide has been arrested at The Willows, apparently while looking for Mr Garibaldi's gemstone. And Kai Slide was located in his flat as he packed his bags ready to flee. The officers have also discovered money under the floorboards and a gold watch. There's no sign of the other valuables we believe have been stolen, but we'll carry on searching. Kai's also being questioned about Fabien's fall. He swears it was an accident. We'll need to talk to Fabien again about that when he's up to it."

"Don't forget Mrs Roberts," Beth had said. "She's got something to do with it all."

"Mrs Roberts?" The officer had flicked through her notebook. "I think we know about her. Mr Garibaldi—' The radio hooked to her lapel had crackled into life and she got to her feet. "I have to go. But you can rest easy – both Bill Slide and Kai are under lock and key."

Jack had let out a breath and turned to Beth in time to receive a big hug, her nose butting against his grazed neck. Her hair had smelt of the apple shampoo she liked to use. Ignoring the pain, he'd allowed himself to relax, and feel all the worry and stress of the last few days ebb away.

In the kitchen now, Jack winced as he tried to get more comfortable in his chair. Exhaustion pounded his body from his skull to his toes. No part of him didn't ache or burn. He glanced over at Mr Garibaldi. He had been close to tears when Jack and Beth had told Fabien's story of Kai threatening him. But now, incredibly, Mr G was cracking jokes and telling of their escape over the rooftops, while Auntie Lil looked increasingly shocked.

Jack switched his attention to the food Auntie Lil had put out. A breadboard, piled with a mound of buttered toast and a long baguette, lay in the centre of the kitchen table, along with jams and cheeses. The last thing Jack felt like was eating, but his belly was hollow and gurgly, so he helped himself to a small slice of toast. Once he started eating, he did feel better. The others tucked in as well. With all the noise of them eating, chatting, retelling stories and interrupting each other, Jack barely registered the doorbell or Auntie Lil getting up to answer it.

"I told Albert to keep a low profile," came a familiar voice from the doorway. "Thank goodness he's all right, but he's got a lot of explaining to do." Mrs Roberts entered and propped herself against the worktop.

Jack stared open-mouthed at Mrs Roberts. Beth bolted from her seat, grabbing the baguette from the breadboard and brandishing it in front of her like a sword. "Stay away from us, you old bat."

"What are you doing?" said Mrs Roberts in horror. "Why do you want to thump me with a stick of bread?"

"Steady on, Beth," said Mr G.

Mrs Roberts inched herself carefully into a spare seat at the table, keeping her eyes on Beth. "Is someone going to tell me what I've missed? Albert?"

"Call the police. She's one of *them*." Beth spat the words out, glaring at Mrs Roberts, the bread still pointing at the old woman's chest.

"We can explain," said Mr G calmly.

"What do you mean, *we*?" said Jack.

"I was trying to tell you on the roof." Mr G lay a hand on Mrs Roberts's arm. "This is my friend, Iris. She's my undercover detective at The Willows."

Beth lowered the bread, but kept it ready in her hand. "*You're* the private detective?"

Mrs Roberts nodded. There was no sign of her deafness now. "Well, I'm semi-retired. Many moons ago, I was a police officer. Then I started my own private detective agency. I've been doing a favour for Albert. I don't take on many clients these days."

The memory of the Mrs Roberts lookalike in Colford last summer flitted through Jack's mind. Maybe it was her after all. Could she have been on a case then?

Mrs Roberts carried on. "I've been investigating Bill Slide at The Willows for the last few weeks, while teaching tai chi."

"Wouldn't it have been better to *live* undercover at The Willows rather than work there?" said Beth, then went pink. "I didn't mean you're . . ."

"I'm not *that* old," said Mrs Roberts, her wrinkles deepening into a frown. "We didn't know if Malcolm or

Nina or anyone else at the home was connected to what was going on. It was crucial that my cover story was believable, and that nobody suspected me."

At the word "believable", Jack choked so hard on his tea Auntie Lil had to thump him on the back. "I saw you in Malcolm's office," Jack eventually spluttered out.

"Really?" Mrs Roberts's eyes widened and she rubbed the back of her neck. "And I thought I'd been so careful."

"You were taking photos . . ." said Beth.

"How do you know that?" Mrs Roberts went crimson.

"I guess you didn't find anything interesting," continued Beth.

"The office was a mess and Malcolm's record-keeping is shoddy," admitted Mrs Roberts.

"So the list *was* a red herring," said Jack.

"What list?" Mrs Roberts shifted her bewildered gaze from Beth to Jack and back again. "The only thing I discovered was a lot of unpaid bills."

"Malcolm has a list of people's valuables in his office." Beth returned the baguette to the breadboard and sat down again, looking less tense.

"Oh dear!" Mrs Roberts's red face went as white as paper. "That might have been mine. During investigations, I found out which of the residents had anything worth stealing and made a list. I must have left it in Malcolm's office when I was searching it."

There was a silence as everyone took in this new piece of information. No wonder, Jack thought, that they'd been suspicious of Mrs Roberts when she'd been so useless as a private detective.

"What we didn't know was how Bill removed the stolen goods from the building," said Mrs Roberts. "You lot have solved that part of the puzzle."

"And I was right, Malcolm's not involved," said Beth triumphantly.

Mr Garibaldi shook his head. "Nor Nina. Iris has been watching them carefully. We don't think they have the faintest idea that Bill is behind the thefts. That slimeball probably started conning people years ago. Iris discovered that a few folks bequeathed small amounts of money to him in their wills. We reckon that's how this all started."

"Did you ask Bill to your place to make a will, so you could suss him out?" Jack asked Mrs Roberts. More things were clicking into place.

Mrs Roberts looked surprised. "You saw that too? You'd make excellent detectives."

"Waiting for people to die is a lengthy business, especially when they're as fit as me," Mr G chuckled.

"Bill started to take bigger risks. He got more impatient, and greedier."

"Is that when you lent a hand with your diamond, Mr G?" said Beth.

Mr Garibaldi puffed out his chest. "I'm not too old to be of use."

Auntie Lil put an arm around his shoulders. "You've been very brave in all of this, Albert. Very brave."

"Yes, Albert created a few rumours for me. He bragged about owning an expensive gemstone, making sure people overheard him. It was a good way to tempt the thief to take more risks, and so make mistakes. And it worked."

"But how did this 'Bill' gain access to people's homes?" asked Auntie Lil.

Mrs Roberts seized a slice of buttered toast. "My theory is that he found out what people had of value when he wrote their wills. Some of them might have even shown him their jewellery when he visited them. Then he popped back at a later date on the pretext of having further questions, did a quick search and grabbed the stuff when they were distracted – making a cup of tea or something. They trusted him, it's as simple as that."

"I had no idea that Fabien was being dragged into it all." Mr Garibaldi wiped a hand over his eyes. "Poor,

poor Fabien. I wish he'd told me about Kai and that he was forcing him to work for him."

Auntie Lil huffed to her feet and pulled an extra plate from a cupboard. "What I don't understand is how you two youngsters got yourselves mixed up in all of this?"

"That's what I'd like to know," said Mrs Roberts, taking the plate from Auntie Lil. Her thatch of grey hair looked wilder than ever.

Jack exchanged a glance with Beth. Obviously, Mrs Roberts didn't know half of what had been going on. But how would they explain . . . ?

Thirty minutes later Jack and Beth had answered the questions Mrs Roberts, Mr Garibaldi and Auntie Lil had thrown at them. Well, most of them. They'd fudged how they'd come to be on the rooftops when they'd first spotted Fabien with the packet of stolen money, by saying that he'd come to them with his troubles. Jack didn't want to imagine the uproar it would cause if everyone found out about their hobby. Shadow jumping was their secret, and Jack wanted it to stay that way. But there was no way of covering up how they'd escaped from The Willows with Mr G. Luckily, Mrs Roberts and Auntie Lil were so in awe of Mr G's ability to climb over the tiles, they didn't question Jack's and Beth's parts too closely.

"Well," said Mrs Roberts, slapping her hands on her knees. "With the evidence the police have found, there's a strong case against Bill and Kai. Enough to lock them up for many years."

"What about Fabien?" asked Mr G suddenly. "Will he be in trouble?"

Mrs Roberts shook her head. "He's young, and Kai coerced him into doing what he did, plus he's been helping the police. I'm sure he'll just get a telling off."

Auntie Lil heaved an enormous sigh. "Well, that's some story, Jack. Thank goodness you've lived to tell the tale. Your mum's not going to be best pleased though."

Mrs Roberts's phone buzzed, and she picked it up and left the room. Jack let out a breath – he didn't even want to think about Mum's "serious conversation", although he was sure it wouldn't be good. Mum-like phrases such as, "How can I trust you when this happens?" and, "What were you thinking?" flitted through his mind. He attempted to push them away while he and the others helped themselves to more food.

Mrs Roberts returned. "Well, that's practically everything wrapped up. According to my contact at the police station, both Bill and Kai have been interviewed and charged. Apparently, the original plan was for Bill to walk out of The Willows with the stolen goods, as bold as you like. He's well-known there, and when he started stealing, security was lax. But he shelved that plan when Malcolm and Nina installed more cameras and Bill got scared of being caught. Kai was very much under Bill's control. Bill ordered him to pick the loot up from the back stairs and carry it away over the rooftops, evading the cameras. Until Kai got spotted by Fabien and panicked. The rest you know." Mrs Roberts sat back at the kitchen table as Auntie Lil placed a cup of tea in front of her. "I have to congratulate you on your storytelling skills, Albert. I don't think Bill would have been as sloppy as he was if it hadn't been for your fake diamond."

"Fake?" Mr Garibaldi grinned at Mrs Roberts, his grey eyes crinkling at the corners. "There's nothing fake about this." He unscrewed his false leg, tipped it upside down and shook a familiar-looking cloth-covered lump onto the table. Slowly, Mr Garibaldi leant forward and unwrapped it, revealing the shimmering, silvery blue stone. Even though Jack had seen it before, it still took his breath away. Everyone was silent, even Mrs Roberts.

Then she let out a long breath. "It's real?" She turned to Mr Garibaldi. "Please explain."

"If you'd known my diamond was real, Iris, you'd never have agreed to me using it as bait. And the story is true," said Mr Garibaldi. "This stone has been passed down the generations of my family. I'm silly not to have put it in a vault somewhere, but with Bill on the take, where better to hide it than in my leg?"

"You certainly pulled the wool over my eyes," said Mrs Roberts.

Everyone passed the gemstone between them. When it came to Jack's turn, he rotated it between the fingers of his good hand, feeling for the second time its solidness, mesmerised by how it gleamed as light bounced off its shiny angled surfaces. "Are you going to tell us now how much it's worth?"

Mr Garibaldi tapped the side of his nose with a bony finger. "That's on a need-to-know basis. And you don't need to know." Jack handed the gem back and Mr G rewrapped it in the handkerchief. "It'll be in the bank vault from now on."

"The important thing is that it's all over. We can breathe easy. It's time to celebrate." Mrs Roberts smiled as she lifted her teacup in the air. "Well done, everyone. Here's to teamwork. Even though we didn't know we were on the same team." She clinked cups with Auntie Lil. "Perhaps it's time I gave up this work and joined you and my sister in Colford . . . I could enjoy a slower pace of life."

"Your sister lives in Colford!" said Jack, his mind turning cartwheels. "So that's what you were doing there last summer . . ." Suddenly, it was like everything was coming into focus.

Mrs Roberts blinked. "Yes, she moved there in August. Why?"

"Doesn't matter," Jack muttered, going hot. He caught Beth's eye and they grinned at each other. Over her shoulder Jack saw more clinking of teacups, and Mr Garibaldi kissing first Mrs Roberts on the cheeks, then Auntie Lil.

Jack let out a breath. Fabien was safe; Mr Garibaldi was alive and kicking. Everyone knew Jack was innocent, and he and Beth were still friends. There was just one more thing Jack had to do, and then everything would be fine.

Chapter Thirty

The next afternoon, the sun was still peeping between the buildings and a burnt orange glow filled the sky, as Jack and Beth picked their way across the Victorian tiles, still slippery from rain the night before. With his bad fingers, Jack would have struggled to climb up onto the roofs from the alleyway without Beth's help, but with a mix of pushing and pulling he'd scrambled onto the lids of the wheelie bins, then onto the flat roof of the warehouse. It always surprised him how strong Beth was.

"I could sleep for a week," she said, as they paused for a rest.

"Me too." At least he had another few days off school to chill out watching Netflix ahead of him. Although now Mum was back home, he was sure she had other plans for him as he was feeling better, starting with a lecture on responsibility. Wasn't saving lives being responsible?

Beth and Jack set off again, slowly navigating the series of ridges and roof valleys towards their favourite view. Jack sighed – it felt like ages since he'd last shadow jumped. Being on the roofs and not able to do it was like having an itch he couldn't scratch. Instead, he had to be content with watching Beth practise a few twists and spins while he shouted tips from the sidelines. It wasn't long before she was too tired to continue, so they clambered up to the final peak and stopped to gaze at the landscape of rooftops stamped across the burning sky. In between the roofs, Jack glimpsed the sand-coloured walls of the cathedral tower, bathed in the golden light of the setting sun. The ornate brickwork shone out against the surrounding darker red and grey buildings of the city. He made out the hospital where Fabien was recovering, and further still the plain block of flats where he lived with Mum. Practically the whole of the city lay in front of them. He'd never grow bored of the view. Not even when he was as old as Mr Garibaldi.

Jack heard Beth sigh beside him. "Wish I could see my home from here, but it's too far out."

"That's the first time I've heard you call Cathy and Pete's place 'home'." Jack realised talking about Cathy and Pete didn't give him the familiar stab of jealousy that it used to.

Beth shrugged. "I guess I'm more comfortable now than I was. Cathy's always saying life's too short to worry about things you can't change. And she's right." Jack cast a glance at her, wondering if Beth was thinking about her parents. "It's cool making a new life for myself with them."

"I thought you might be fed up with hanging out with me. Now you've got them, and Sadie too," he mumbled.

"What? No chance. Cathy and Pete have been fantastic to me since Mum and Dad died. But it doesn't mean I don't want to spend time with you. Anyway . . ." Beth nudged him with an elbow. "You've got other friends too."

Jack frowned. "Like who? I'm the person everyone avoids because of this." He pointed at the greasy skin on his face which, even though the sun had almost set, was coated in a thick layer of cream to prevent any burning.

"Fabien for one," she said firmly. "Or do you just feel sorry for him?"

"Course not." Jack took in her words as he leant against the crumbling chimney stack. Fabien – who he'd spent lunchtimes with in the school library, who'd come to his place to play video games. Who he'd seen lying unconscious in a hospital bed. Whose life he'd helped save on the rooftops. The boy who reminded Jack of himself. She was right. Fabien *was* his friend, and he hadn't really noticed.

"It's always fun hanging out with you," Beth said. "Even if we've been accused of stealing and chased around a retirement home, not to mention practically falling off a roof with an old man with one leg and a sick boy who's scared of heights."

He chuckled. "When you put it like that . . ."

Beth huffed, ruffling her fringe with her breath. "I'm glad Malcolm's not a thief. Nina too, even though she's been a cow to us. But how could Bill be such a slimeball?"

Jack shrugged. "Some people get obsessed with money." From their vantage point he spotted flashing blue lights as a police car zoomed past far below. It made him think of Bill and Kai, safely locked up. Jack was glad *he* didn't have an uncle like Bill.

Beth's phone beeped. She glanced at it, grinned and showed Jack. He read it and laughed. It was a message from Fabien, still in hospital. Now Jack had lost his phone, Fabien had to send messages to Beth to pass on to Jack. *Gonna give me shadow jumping lessons?*

"Are you going to do it?" asked Beth.

Jack grinned. "Why not?" He tapped a message back. *Sure. You need them.* Fabien replied a few seconds later with a photo of himself sitting in bed with a big smile on his face, wearing his beanie hat, and making a thumbs up gesture. Despite everything that had happened, the idea of teaching Fabien some moves made Jack happy. Happy to share his space with his friend, his *two* friends. Jack grinned again, stuffing his good hand into the warmth of his hoodie pocket. His fingers closed around something. "Hey, I've got this for you." Jack brought out Beth's chain and locket.

"You found my heart!" Her chin wobbled.

"Yeah, I guessed that it probably dropped when you were hanging over the parapet. I went back and found it lying in the gutter in the street below." He didn't mention he'd got up at the crack of dawn to search for it before the sun got too high. It had taken ages to find.

"Thanks a lot." Beaming from ear to ear, Beth looped it around her neck. "You're a great mate."

Jack went hot with embarrassment. What more proof did he need that she was his friend? He'd been acting like a prize idiot – feeling left out, moping because Beth didn't do the stuff he wanted her to do. There was nothing wrong with her wanting her own space.

Jack felt a warm hand pressing into his own, Beth's fingers entwining with his. They stood side by side on the ridge of the roof, looking towards the cathedral tower. He glanced across at her. A wisp of stray black hair blew across her cheek, and she scraped it back, tucking it behind her ear. She was staring into the distance, her lips pinched together against the sharp breeze.

"So, what shall we do now?" she asked.

He grinned, liking that she said "we". "Shadow jumping's probably out, right?"

"With your injuries? No chance," Beth said, grinning back. "Won't be long though."

"Can't wait." And with Jack's good hand in hers, they jogged down the slope and into the shadows, away from the setting sun.

Post a review!

Let me know what you thought of *Twilight Robbery* by visiting **jm-forster.com** and filling in the contact form or by posting a review with your favourite online retailer.

You can also join my mailing list on my website to keep up-to-date with my news.

jm-forster.com

Also by J. M. Forster

Shadow Jumper: a mystery adventure for children and young teens. Available in paperback, ebook and audio download.

Bad Hair Days: a touching mystery about family, friendships and being different. Available in paperback and ebook. Perfect for older children and young teens.

Acknowledgements

To Giles, Ben and Louis, for being there. To my Cheltenham Critique Group, for encouragement, conversation and honest feedback. To Helene at The Suffolk Anthology bookshop, Cheltenham, UK, for supporting independent authors and providing us with a meeting space. To members of the Alliance of Independent Authors, for answering my questions on all things publishing.

About the Author

J. M. Forster is an award-winning writer of books for older children and young teens. She lives in Gloucestershire, UK, with her husband, two lovely sons and Frodo, the Australian labradoodle. *Twilight Robbery* is her third novel. Her first novel, *Shadow Jumper,* won Gold Award in the Wishing Shelf Book Awards 2014. *Bad Hair Days* was a finalist in the Wishing Shelf Book Awards 2017.

Twilight Robbery